Praise for Jaycee Clark's *Black Aura*

Rating: 5 Angels "Black Aura is an incredible story that will keep you guessing until the very end. ...Readers, you will not want to miss Black Aura because you are in for a spine-tingling treat."

~ *Contessa, Fallen Angel Reviews*

Rating: 5 Blue Ribbons "Jaycee Clark is back and what a rush. BLACK AURA is a brilliant follow up to ANGEL EYES, not only has Ms. Clark carried on with her tension filled, nail biting suspenseful settings but with her knack for giving us characters who will live on in our memories for a long time to come – reader will no doubt be adding this one their library."

~ *jhayboy, Romance Junkies*

Rating: 4 Hearts "These are interesting characters and the author does a marvelous job concealing the villain's identity while building the malevolent suspense."

~ *Lynn, The Romance Studio*

Rating: 5 Hearts "....Ms. Clark has the knack of keeping you guessing right to the end. Suspense and the paranormal, two of my favourite genres together, written by an awesome writer, this must be heaven!"

~ *Valerie, Love Romances and More*

"Jaycee Clark has written an exciting series that I hope will continue with Alyssa."

~ *Nanette, Joyfully Reviewed*

Look for these titles by
Jaycee Clark

Now Available:

Angel Eyes

Talons Anthology: Firebird

Print Anthology

Talons

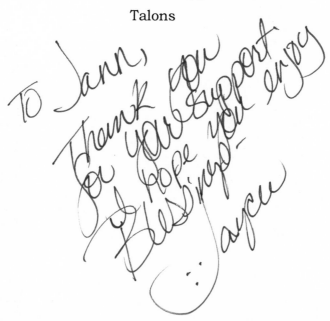

Black Aura

Jaycee Clark

A Samhain Publishing, Ltd. publication.

Samhain Publishing, Ltd.
577 Mulberry Street, Suite 1520
Macon, GA 31201
www.samhainpublishing.com

Black Aura
Copyright © 2009 by Jaycee Clark
Print ISBN: 978-1-60504-413-2
Digital ISBN: 1-59998-504-7

Editing by Deborah Nemeth
Cover by Scott Carpenter

First Samhain Publishing, Ltd. electronic publication: December 2008
First Samhain Publishing, Ltd. print publication: October 2009

Dedication

This book is dedicated to dreamers who believe in themselves even when they question their sanity for doing so. Also, thanks to Kristie for reading through this and for listening to crazy ideas. A big thanks to my last minute readers: Patti and Cindy. And Deb, a wonderful editor who thankfully didn't kill me, even though she probably wanted to.

Prologue

He hissed as the pain snaked through his system, dark and biting. The medication slithered in its wake, waiting, sneaking, swallowing the pain whole.

It wasn't enough. Never enough.

He couldn't feel it anymore, couldn't feel the fast, humming energy that had always charged through him, that *sustained* him.

He needed another transfer. Transfers charged him. They did more than any medical treatments ever did. He knew that, felt it, *believed* it.

Death for all was only a matter of time. He was hardly stupid, he knew time was measured, limited. But he believed he could push back the inevitable given enough time, just a bit more. Perhaps one day he'd find the *one*, the right one who would take all the pain away, make all the sickness disappear.

Make him better.

Heal him.

Not that he hadn't been to see the local healer. He had. Hell, he'd tracked others down, known healers, and all said the same. Doctors were of no real use to him. They rarely believed, even if they claimed they did. The energy that had always coursed through him, gifted him, blessed him, now seemed to be his curse.

He *needed* the energy. To survive he'd have to have the transfers, must have them as beings needed air.

Just any transfer would not do. He needed special ones, and now he had to find who would be next. On a sigh, he thought of the young virgin, whose body he'd left out in the woods where no one would find it. She would be missed, it was inevitable. He wondered idly if her family had known how truly special she had been. Had she even been reported as missing yet? He'd taken her fast. Fast and furiously. The transfer had been there, yes, but it had lacked...something.

She had been so easy, giving off that air of vulnerability. He breathed deeply. How he loved the vulnerable. They were so easy to lead... Special ones, especially the younger, were so easily manipulated. She had had no idea what her visions and gifts truly were. Her parents had her medicated for whatever it was the latest doctor had assured them she'd been afflicted with. After two suicide attempts it was doubtful any would immediately think she was really missing, and if they did find her body, posed just so, would anyone ask any questions?

Probably. If she was found before the animals got to her, it would be hard to miss the marks on her neck. Strangling someone took more strength than most people thought. Either way, he'd helped her achieve what she wanted, hadn't he? She hadn't really wanted to live, so he'd helped her in a sense.

Helped her as she'd helped him. She'd given to him that which he'd needed.

Her energy.

The energy transfer hadn't been the largest surge in power he'd ever experienced. But then she hadn't wanted to live as others had. He had already learned that the more gifted usually wanted to live, thrived to live, had an intricate, primeval force to *live.* Those were the strongest transfers. Hers had been bright, yet shadowed at the same time, a charge quickly over with only a minor hum after her last breath, her being, her essence had been transferred to him.

They were all special. But he needed *more*, needed them and quickly. He needed a strong one. One who wanted to live. Maybe to find the stronger, he'd have to look at more mature women, not those who were so young. The young after all often believed themselves to be invincible, didn't they? Often thought nothing bad could ever truly happen to them. To the young, it was always someone else who overdosed, who died in car accidents or was abducted, abused or killed. Even so, there was something very special about taking those younger ones, those conflicted and at a point where they could choose their own path—good or bad.

He breathed deeply and relished the memory of youth, of their scent, of their innocence.

He needed his gifted ones to be strong, not just slightly gifted, not just a little special. *Powerful.*

Strong.

He looked in the mirror. His pale face, sunken eyes stared back at him.

He had to find the next one—and quickly.

Chapter One

She'd run away.

Which was completely unlike her. She hated, absolutely hated failure.

Lake Johnson shifted in the chilled early morning air, tinged with smoke and tickling pine. She could also smell snow on the air, as if the low-hanging clouds obscuring Taos Mountain were not enough of an indication.

Chicken.

She stood on the sidewalk, outside the art gallery across the street from the loft she was renting. The gallery's rusted metal sign over the door, *Symbols,* made her wonder exactly what it meant to everyone. Symbols was a popular gallery, judging by all the traffic it saw. She'd been inside it more than once, but not because she really liked everything in it. Some of the sculptures were weird, though she loved the sepia prints done of local landscapes, slightly skewed in some graphic design program, probably. Either way, some of the stuff called to her.

Or maybe someone.

Go in. Just go in and ask him.

No.

Taking a deep breath she looked around, tapping her nails

on her thigh. Maybe she should have had another cup of coffee. But then the cup of coffee was a problem. The owner of the damned coffee shop was one of the reasons she stood here contemplating asking the sexy gallery owner, Maxamillan Gray, out on a date.

Once upon a time she wouldn't have thought twice about asking a guy out. But that was before. Before her life had been tossed into chaos. Before she started to second-guess herself.

Which was why she'd spent the winter here in Taos, New Mexico. Why she was still hiding here when she owned her own new age shop and other property in Sedona, Arizona. At least she wasn't hurting for money. Which was a good thing, considering she needed a reasonable excuse for coming into the gallery yet again. Maybe today she'd spend some of that money...on...something?

Guts and glory. Just open the door, look around and ask him out.

Lake scanned the crowd again. The locals, or who she thought of as locals, were out and about. She glanced across the street to see Mr. Howard, the owner of the coffee shop and her landlord. The coffee bar sat on a main street, lined with more galleries, stores, and restaurants than most passing-through travelers cared to appreciate. The old streets were lined with historical adobe buildings. The streets were also narrow, so traffic on any given weekend and most weekdays was a real bitch, she'd learned, but that was okay too. There were worse things in life than sitting on her little deck above the coffee shop and watching the tourists piss each other off as they tried to maneuver through the old town shadowed by mountains, pueblos and Native American history.

Mr. Howard waved to her. Wiley, old matchmaking bastard. He knew she watched the gallery, must have sensed she liked the owner, because this morning with her cup of coffee he'd served her the idea that Maxamillan was interested in her. He'd *asked* about her.

So if he was interested, then why didn't she wait for the guy to ask her out, and what the hell was she doing standing on the sidewalk arguing with herself? These days however, she second-guessed herself all the damned time.

She didn't know if she could read people correctly anymore.

Once upon a time she'd read people, made a fine living running her shop focused around readings and tarot and auras. That had been before. Before she'd had the misfortune of thinking she fell for a guy who was not what he'd seemed. The bastard had almost killed her best friend, and she had not even seen it until it was almost too late.

Now, months later, she still second-guessed herself. She could still read people, could still read auras, but could she *trust* those readings?

As she watched, one person she knew she did read correctly strode down the sidewalk towards her. The young woman—Lake figured in her late teens or early twenties—was troubled. Her aura was damaged, dark and muted, but Lake could see where it had once been bright, shining and shifting, a rainbow dancing on water. Energies trailed behind her, like long tendrils, reaching across the street even. Anger, pain, hope, and...hope.

Lake wondered again who the young woman was. She'd seen her go into the shop before, though she'd never been in the gallery when Lake had visited.

Chicken.

Shut up.

The waiting isn't getting easier.

"Fine." She pulled her tote higher on her shoulder, one she'd knitted from fun yarn of various colors. It was bright, cheery and probably ugly to some. She loved it.

To hell with it. Just go in. Look around. Ask him. One. Two. Three.

Lake pushed into the gallery just after the young woman, who looked back twice before stepping into the shop as well. Up close, Lake noticed the girl had wise eyes.

The shop smelled as it had the other times she'd been in, a mixture of hardwood and turpentine. The pale terracotta-washed walls were a great backdrop for the black-framed prints. Two walls were covered in photographs, black and whites, sepias. The other held various sized canvasses, bold slashes of paints, sweeping landscapes, cool watercolors. Everything was showcased, from neoclassical to more modern, darker works. A bank of windows filtered in the light splashing onto pedestals and display cases with everything from sculptures to jewelry. She'd been in several times to look around, so maybe no one would think anything of her being in here now.

The girl glanced at the man, Maxamillan Gray, behind the counter and then at Lake. Lake saw then, the girl was an old soul.

Smiling, the young woman said in a soft voice, "You know you're yellow?"

"Alyssa," Maxamillan warned.

Lake studied him, as attracted to him as she always seemed to be. He was a bit taller than her, and she topped or stood even to most men at five foot eleven. On the occasion she managed to drag her ass out of bed for early morning Pilates, she'd seen the man cycling or jogging. Long and lithe, he was toned but not muscular. His forearms and biceps attested to all the sculpting he did. Some might think him soft, she supposed. After all, he wasn't the rugged cowboy, nor was he the suave

New York gallery owner. This was a man who lived and owned his own world and was very proud of that fact. He wore no ring, with no signs he'd worn one recently, which didn't actually mean anything.

His gray eyes landed on her and raked her over quickly once, then narrowed slightly at the corners before slowly gazing down her body again. When his gaze met her eyes, she cocked a brow and gave him one of her half grins.

Maxamillan's dark hair was dusted with gray at the temples. His chiseled face was neither too narrow, nor overly harsh. He reminded her of a David sculpture—perfection from his slightly curled hair to his lips, the bottom slightly plumper than the top.

And where the hell was her mind? The look, the gaze, those lips and the way he moved. She knew enough about men to know he'd be great in bed. Or maybe she just *knew*.

A slight blush stole over his cheekbones before he turned back to the young girl. "Alyssa, you owe this woman an apology."

Lake refocused on the young woman—dark hair, cut short and stylish, her eyes the same gray as Maxamillan's—and realized they were related.

"Dad."

Lake grinned, seeing the tattoo on the girl's shoulder, a Celtic symbol. "Actually—Alyssa, is it?—I've always seen my aura as more orange than yellow. But then, granted I've been out of sorts for the last several months, so yellow is probably right. Come to think of it, I'm surprised it's not blue or brown or something." She studied the young woman and dropped her shields, barely tapping into the energies surrounding them. "You, on the other hand, used to be all colors." The energy all but poured over her. "My God."

Alyssa frowned. "Whatever."

The power shooting off the girl started to tap and drain her own. The anger was spiked. Not anger—no—rage. Rage, dark and deadly in its repression, all but hissed in the air. It was held in check by the calming waters of hope, of blue, of greens, of...

Lake could only stare at the young troubled woman. "No. I-I saw before, the muted colors, but I had no idea..." She had to push the energy charging across her skin back, back behind the shields. She took a deep breath and looked square into Alyssa's gray eyes. "You are an incredibly, incredibly gifted young woman. I hope you know that." Then other words tumbled out of her mouth. "Be careful. Be very, very careful, Alyssa."

Alyssa stared at her a moment more, shook her head and then turned without another word and walked to the back of the gallery.

Lake watched her, heard the boots thumping on the scarred wooden floor, even heard the faint jingle of the bling on the girl's low-slung jeans.

A door in the back slammed.

Lake blinked and remembered where she was and what she'd done. "Oh my God. I'm sorry. I just..." She trailed off. "I shouldn't have..."

Maxamillan cleared his throat, looking in the direction his daughter had gone. "Actually, it's okay. She loves to shock people, thinks it's great fun. Fact is, she's not used to the tables being turned." He pushed the sleeves of his long sleeved Henley up. The light gray brought out the color of his eyes. "She's always thought..." Those eyes speared her. "Well, it doesn't matter."

Lake studied him and realized that perhaps he didn't know.

"You do realize your daughter is very gifted? I haven't seen or felt energies like hers in years."

One brow arched. "You believe in auras?"

Lake couldn't help it. She laughed. Digging in her purse, she pulled out a card with her name and cell on it. Then she pointed across the way to the coffee shop. "Give this to your daughter. Tell her to come see me. I own—or did own, and probably will own again...well, actually, I do plan to reopen up when I move back..." She realized she was rambling. "I do own a shop in Sedona."

He grinned at her. "Are you sure about that? You sound like you might not have it figured out yet."

"Yes, I'm sure."

"What type of shop?" He glanced at the card, then back at her. "A shop for all your needs?"

"A new age shop. That's my slogan." Shaking off the feeling she needed to explain herself to him, she continued, "Anyway, tell her I'm staying over there and to call me if she wants to..." Again she trailed off. "Talk."

He frowned and scratched the side of his face, studying her card. "You're staying over at the coffee shop?"

"Renting a room from the Howards." She wished now she hadn't worn the turtleneck sweater. It was warm. Or maybe it was just her. "It's a nice place. The H-Howards are really nice." She was rambling. Jeez.

"Oh-kay. Well, Lake." His gaze rose back to hers. "Your name is really Lake?"

She rolled her eyes. "Is yours really Maxamillan?"

He laughed. "Touché. Though, please call me Max."

"Max." Lake smiled, turned and walked to the door.

Just as her hand touched the old rusted handle, he said,

"Um, look. I've seen you over there, seen you come in a few times and I was wondering..."

Lake stopped and stared back at him. Waited. And waited some more. She hoped to hell he wasn't in a relationship.

"And you were wondering...?"

"That is, well," he muttered something and took a breath. "I was wondering if you'd like to go for drinks sometime."

She smiled. "I'm really not into the bar scene, Max."

He frowned. "Neither am I."

"Good. Then how about the coffee shop?"

He smiled and the corners of his eyes crinkled up. "I'd like that."

She waited.

"This evening around..." He motioned with his hand. "Seven?"

"Sounds good. See you at seven across the street, Max."

Just as she walked through the door she heard, "'Bout time. God, Dad, I thought you'd never actually spit it out."

Chapter Two

Now what the hell was she going to wear?

A closet full of clothes. She had them, plenty to choose from. She'd rummaged and pawed through the outfits, skirts, shirts, pants looking for *the* outfit, but it was like freaking geometry. Nothing was congealing. The short purple skirt? Or the long purple skirt? The purple velvet dress? The hangers screeched over the rod and she realized she didn't have a broad rainbow in her wardrobe.

Black.

Black.

Purple.

Blue.

White.

Black.

Granted with her red hair, it wasn't like she wore scarlet— or God forbid pink—but yellow would be nice. Tonight she'd like a lovely golden...something.

And not a burst of sunshine in the whole damn closet. At least she had a sexy golden lace lingerie set. *Not* that she was looking to get laid, at least not yet. An image of Max popped into her head, the grace and ease of his movements. Then again, if getting laid tonight was in the cards, she might just go along with it.

So what the hell to wear? Of course, she could go buy something, but that put too much importance on a casual date.

And lingerie didn't?

It was casual, wasn't it? Or was it more? Should she dress it up? Keep it simple? Had he really wanted to ask her out or had he been on the spot?

The landlord's deep voice rumbled up through the open balcony door. What if the Howards had said something to Maxamillan? Then said something to her? Then he'd felt compelled to ask her?

She was losing her mind.

What if he made a habit of taking out girls who were renting from the Howards?

What if he was an ax murderer?

Frowning, she grabbed her cell phone and dialed her closest friend, Cora. Why couldn't she be more like Cora? Even after almost dying, Cora had her life more together than she did.

"Hello, Mystic Moons. How can I help you?" Cora's voice floated over the phone all cheery and calm.

"Why is it always an ax murderer?"

A silent pause.

"Lake?"

"Why an ax murderer? Why the hell doesn't anyone ever say, 'Oh, he could be a deadly arsonist'? Or—or, why don't they say, 'You just never know, he could be a KGB assassin'?"

Another pause. "Ummm...the KGB's no longer an issue? He'd be really old then, and I'm going to take a wild guess here that this is about a guy who can't be old enough to worry about KGB assassins or he'd be our father's age—which I suppose is okay, if you're okay with that, but you like them younger."

There were few people who could keep up with her.

"Then why doesn't anyone say, 'He could be an armed terrorist'?"

"Versus as unarmed one? Yes, I always thought they were so much sexier unarmed." Something rustled in the background. "What are you talking about? What guy? Have you finally asked out the gallery owner?"

She sighed and sat on the bed. Cora knew all her secrets. "He asked me out and I have nothing to wear."

"Smart man. I've no idea what's taken you so long. I was starting to worry you were going to become some pagan fanatic forswearing men and sex."

"Bite thou tongue."

Cora laughed. "I'm betting he'll bite yours later if you ask him really nicely—with or without you wearing anything. Nothing to wear? You've got more clothing than anyone I know. Yes, I'm sure he'd be hugely disappointed if you showed up naked. That would just ruin all those artistic thoughts I'm certain he's been having about you."

Clothing lay scattered across the bed—the remains of a deranged woman blasting her closet. She picked up a blue crushed-velvet dress. No, not that one, not that one either.

"You're not helping. I need something to wear and I have nothing but water colors."

"Kinky. Did you paint them on, or did he? I must come visit this gallery of his."

Lake laughed. "Help me. You're supposed to be helping here. I need help."

"This is not news to me. You've always needed help, honey. Acceptance is the first step. Now we have hope."

"I'm hanging up now."

Cora's laugh warmed her. "I miss you. When are you coming home?"

Lake sighed, still horrified by what had happened months before when her abilities had failed to read true evil. An evil that had almost cost Cora her life. Could she ever go back?

"I don't know, Cora."

For a minute Cora said nothing, then tsked. "It wasn't your fault. How many times do we have to go through this? No one blames you."

"Maybe not, but that doesn't stop me from blaming myself." Or questioning her own abilities about reading people. "Nothing like sleeping with a serial killer to make you question yourself."

"Sorry, forget I asked," Cora said. "Just take your time. Things are fine here. Oh and I went over and grabbed some of your stock to sell here while you're on your sabbatical. I hated to think of everything just collecting dust. I marked it up twenty percent, then put 'on sale' and took off ten percent, and I'll keep the other ten and you still get your regular prices for things."

Lake smiled. "Good business brain. If you hadn't marked things up, I'd have come over there and told you to close shop because you didn't have the brains to make any money." She shifted back against the raw pine headboard and stared at the *latilla* ceiling. The walls were bare of all but a few strategically placed southwestern artworks. Koki eternally played his flute. She was starting to get tired of the curved flute player. And she missed color, there just wasn't a whole lot of color here in the décor. "So tell me how things are going."

"Where do I even start?"

"You and Rogan okay?"

Cora chuckled. "Great. He wants to get married."

"And this is news to you how?"

"Shut up. I haven't answered."

Lake laughed. "Making him wait for something, that's almost cruel of you. You've been keeping secrets." She listened as Cora filled her in on things she'd been missing.

Cora sighed. "Soooo tell me about the gallery owner and why you're stressing about what to wear. Date? Casual or hoping-for-more? Dinner?"

"I've decided on the long slinky rust dress." Lake picked up the amethyst pendant between her breasts and ran it along the chain as she studied the closet. Shoes. Which shoes?

"Very classy with a hint of sexy yet is conservative and both casual or dressy. Very good. Wear your purple wrap if you have it. And the amethyst pendant."

Lake smiled. "I really miss you." In the background she heard the tinkling chime of bells, which she recognized as the shop bell in Cora's Mystic Moons.

"I've got to go, sweetie, take care. And I want the deets in the morning."

"Blow by blow?"

"Only if you've learned some long-buried secret about a technique."

"Well, I'm sure I could come up with something," Lake told her.

"Not that many deets, no. Have fun. Be safe. You got a safe number? Someone know where you'll be?"

"Downstairs in the coffee shop drinking espresso and eating biscotti."

"Morning, deets. You don't call, and I can't get a hold of you, Rogan and I will be driving to Taos and banging on your door."

"On the door? Please, at least be inside before you start giving the poor neighbors a sight they'd never forget."

Cora laughed. "I'm hanging up now."

"Shoes?"

"Now we enter unknown territory and I shall go. Love you. Take care and I mean it, call me in the morning so I know you're okay."

"I will. Love you too, tell everyone I said hello."

As she shut her cell phone, she dug in the closet and got out everything she needed, hanging it on the closet door.

God, she was tired. She really needed to start sleeping better.

"You're not wearing that, are you?" his daughter asked him from the doorway of his room.

Max looked at his reflection. Black pants, black shoes, black shirt and jacket. Matching, practical and classic. "No, I thought I'd wait until I got to the door and strip down to my hot pink Speedos."

"Oh God, I need therapy now." Alyssa covered her eyes and muttered, "Stab out my third eye."

He grinned as he turned and studied his daughter. Running a hand over his shirt front, he asked, "You really think this won't work?"

She opened her eyes and leaned against the doorframe. A cool breeze blew through the apartment from the open front windows and she rubbed her bare arms. Her style he would never understand. She never stuck to any one thing. At present it was what he referred to as her hip-careless-goth look. A black tank over a dark maroon tank, her dusty jeans, hair standing up, accessorized with sparkling bling mixed with skull bling. Somehow she made it all work together. At least she didn't do the death-white face and black lips or nail polish. So he'd keep his opinions on her wardrobe to himself with the knowledge that tomorrow could be the preppy-cowgirl look. At nineteen she was moody and petulant, hopeful and funny and still too quiet for his peace of mind. Her eyes were never clear of nightmares or troubles, and she rarely smiled that big dimpled smile he remembered always on her face as a child.

After the accident that claimed his ex-wife and son, he'd decided life was too precious to worry about the small stuff, like Alyssa's clothing. Sweat dampened his skin at the mere memory of his daughter hooked to tubes and monitors, not knowing at first if she'd live or die. Then the months of therapy here, their rocky beginning...

He sighed and shook off the dark thoughts.

Today was good. Alyssa was good and at least joking, even if he wished she ate a bit more. Not a petite woman, she should have more meat on her bones and her diet was atrocious. At least she was eating, even if it was junk food. None of these things he would mention tonight, as he didn't want a tirade before he left to meet Lake.

Yet her staying healthy was important.

"What will you have for dinner?" he dared.

"A marshmallow."

"Nutritious and fun at the same time," he added dryly.

"Well, I thought if I added dark chocolate and raspberry jam I'd get some fruit and helpful vitamins and antioxidants, which are good for you." She crossed her arms and studied him. "You really need some color in your wardrobe."

"This coming from the girl who wore only black and gray for the first three months of living here."

"I'm Kettle so I'm supposed to point out the obvious, Pot. It's a rule, it's clichéd."

"You're annoying and irritating, but I love you."

Alyssa's sigh huffed across the room. "Maybe a dark red tie? A dark silver one? No, that's no color." She straightened. "I know." With that she walked to his closet and rummaged through his ties.

"I don't want to wear a damn tie. It's coffee."

She stopped and tilted her head. "You're right. That would take the casualness out of it. Maybe..." Her hands quickly sorted through his shirts. "There!" She pulled out a dark purple silk shirt. "Wear this with the black jacket. You're still the dark moody artist, no yellow, no pumpkin orange."

"God forbid."

She shrugged. "Could be worse, pink."

"You'll know I've gone off the deep end if ever there is pink in my closet."

She waggled the hanger at him.

Max took the shirt, heading to the bathroom.

"And we've already gone over the safe-sex speech before. You still have condoms?"

He froze, her words tumbling in his brain. Speechless, he could only stare at her. He opened his mouth, shut it, and then frowning, opened it again. Shaking his head, he shut the door.

Alyssa's voice traveled through the wood. "You know if you have any questions—"

"I sure as hell won't be asking you." He jerked off the shirt he'd chosen, changing into the one Alyssa had handed him, fumbling with the buttons. Sex advice from his kid? Legal and grown kid? Still his kid. He took a deep breath and stared at his reflection in the mirror while he said, "You're—you're nineteen."

Legal or not, there were just certain things fathers should never...

"So? Sex today is different than sex when you were nineteen."

He knew better than to ask, but it was so absurd. He'd survived the disco age, the flashing eighties for God's sake. "Really? And here I thought some things were basic."

He tucked in the bottom of his shirt. She was right, this looked better.

"Safe sex, Dad. There are diseases and things you should worry about now. Talking about important issues often makes them second nature. Safe sex, no to drugs and always put on clean underwear."

Max opened the bathroom door and stared at her.

She grinned and wiggled her brows.

Shock. She loved to shock.

"Maybe Lake will like my pink Speedos."

"Ewww...I'm leaving now." She hurried from the room.

Max laughed as he put on his watch. He wondered what the long, leggy, built-like-an-Irish-goddess woman would be wearing tonight.

Lake—strange name. Different. Original. Unique.

Rather like the woman.

The coffee shop hummed with the evening crowd. Lake wondered how they stayed open as long as they did. The

Howards were up at dawn or before—the smell of baking treats always woke her up, mixing with the heady scent of Arabica beans. She chose a table near the front windows.

"Is this table fine?" she asked Max. "If you smoke we can sit out on the back patio." Nothing like cigarette smoke mixing with coffee, spices and cinnamon to bring one awake in the mornings. To each their own.

"This table is fine. And just for the record, I don't smoke."

As they sat, she looked across the little iron table at Max. Dressed in dark plum and black, he looked good enough to lick. And here she was in her purple wrap and copper gown. At least she hadn't gone with the black dress or they could have looked like Ken and Barbie. Coordinating outfits and as it was, they already...already...fit, she decided. They fit just a little too well. When he'd pulled her chair out for her, the warmth of his hand just above the base of her spine zinged excitement through her. Goose bumps again pricked her skin just at the memory.

His eyes perused her, catalogued her features, not as a man deciding on whether or not he liked what he saw—hell, she knew enough about males to know that he liked what saw. No, it was the subtle appreciation in his eyes that gave her pause. He studied her like the art aficionado he was, as if she were some rare painting or sculpture he wanted to memorize.

She smiled and he blinked.

"Sorry, I'm staring aren't I?" he asked, shifting to lean back and sip his little cup of espresso. Biscotti lay to the side on a small blue pottery plate.

She tapped a nail on the side of her café mocha. "Yes."

"Sorry," he said again, the edges of his eyes crinkling.

"It's okay. I'd let you know if I thought it was creepy."

One brow arched. "And it isn't?"

Lake sighed and let the wrap slide down to her elbows. "I know creepy." At least she thought she did. "No, it's more like..." She thought about her words. "It's more like you're trying to figure out which colors to use on a canvas, or what medium you'd like to use."

The right corner of his mouth edged up. "Then can I stop worrying about how to ask you if you'd like to model for me?"

It was her turn to grin and lean up on the table. "You want me to model for you?"

He leaned up as well, those intense eyes scanning her face before they met hers straight on, heat in their depths. "In this day and age, most women are too skinny, or let themselves go too much. Around here in Taos, you've got tourists, the local health freaks, and those who don't care. There are few who fit the balance perfectly."

She moved her hand closer to his on the table. "Balance. You're a Libra."

"I'm that easy?"

She laughed and shook her head. "Easy? If you were easy, Max, I'd have asked you out weeks and weeks ago, instead of stressing about it."

"Yeah, well, I like balance. I don't do chaos very well, but perfect order drives me nuts."

"Me, too."

"You a Libra as well?"

She tilted her head. "We'll wait on me. So you want me to model for you?"

"Ohhh yeah," he drew out.

"Why?"

"You remind me of a goddess."

She gave him a long blink. Something must be wrong with

this guy. A goddess? There was a line she hadn't heard before. For a moment words failed her.

"Goddess? I'm no goddess." Then she smiled. A goddess. Butterflies danced in her stomach. She wasn't that easy, was she? Touching his hand with hers, she again felt that charged hum between them. Not a bright burst of energy like she'd had with others—like heated passion that could quickly burn out. Nor the electric bolt of pure sex and just sex. This was different.

With Max, all those charges were there, but not. It was as if those feelings were there, but all rolled together so that the hum was a twisted, intertwined cable, coating and protecting the current. She'd never experienced this before and she was honest enough to know she wanted to feel more.

"You're different," she whispered.

His brows wiggled and he smiled, a wicked smile that left her wondering what he was thinking.

For a moment they only stared at each other.

"So are you," he answered, his voice low and caressing. He broke eye contact and glanced at their coffees sitting between them. "This has been fun, but I'm hungry. You want to go eat?"

That was such a loaded question, but she let it go. The twinkle in his eyes said he heard her thoughts.

"You like spice?" he asked, leaning even closer towards her.

Her gaze dropped from his eyes to his lips. What would they feel like on her? She'd bet he knew how to use his mouth. "I uh..." She frowned. "Spice? As in 'and everything nice'?"

"I sincerely hope not."

"Yeah, same here."

That corner of his mouth edged sexily up again. "As in hot. Food."

"Food." Food.

His flash of teeth made her want to bite him.

She sat back, quickly. What the hell was wrong with her? For months she'd been celibate. Granted she'd thought about...okay, maybe *fantasized* once or twice about Max. But this? This was *fast*. This was fast and furious and she wondered, *what the hell*. Had she learned nothing?

"What?" he asked.

It wasn't fair to paint him with the black brush and poisoned paint that her last fling had left her with. Taking a deep breath, she closed her eyes, centered on herself and tried to...*feel*. She missed feeling, knowing what was what, not only around her, but within herself.

To hell with it.

She opened her eyes and focused on Max. "Nothing. Spicy food is fine."

His narrowed eyes watched her. Did the man miss anything, because it sure as hell didn't feel like it.

As they stood, he opened his wallet. She put her hand on his arm. "I sort of roped you into this."

The straight-on stare stopped her even before his words. "I don't let women pay. Period. You have a problem with that?"

Men were so damned touchy. If she said no, she sounded like she wanted a sugar daddy and if she said yes, she sounded ungrateful. She shrugged. "Whatever you want."

They headed for the door, his hand again on the base of her spine. Not just to pull her chair out, but to guide her around the other tables through the dimly lit coffee shop to the door. At the register sat the Howard's lanky son, Mark. He attended the local college, but then two of their three sons were enrolled at Northern New Mexico Community College. The young man's eyes, bright and blue, followed her and Max across the shop to the door. He glanced across the street and then ducked his head.

What in the world?

Outside, on the sidewalk, the chilled evening air danced over her and she shivered.

Max looked up and down the street. "We could go to Mario's—great Italian."

"I know. I love their marsala."

"Or we could go to Benita's. Great New Mexican food."

She grinned. "Either one, though I have to say that I love New Mexican food, the subtle flavors, spicy but not red chili spicy, ya know?"

"Yes, I know." He frowned and looked at his watch. "I should have made reservations."

She shrugged. "It's okay. It's spur of the moment."

"Fulfilled hope is a better term."

"Ah." She liked this. This excitement mixed with anxiety. "Let's walk." She held her hand out to him and he took it after only a moment's pause, his warm and comforting.

"It's cold tonight."

"Snow's coming back," she agreed.

Her heels clicked along the sidewalk, and they moved to the side to let a group of college students by, or maybe just a group of young friends.

As they made the three-block walk to Benita's, neither said very much. However, it wasn't the normal awkward silence of many first dates, it was more the comfortable silence of friends.

They neared the restaurant and she could see they wouldn't be eating, at least sitting down to dine, anytime soon.

"Well, damn," Max muttered.

"Carry-out?" she asked, and then realized that might be

read as—

"Works for me."

Stop worrying, for crying out loud, she thought. He was nice, she'd watched him for months. His aura was a calming blue, with the occasional color burst. But that was normal, at least to her, for very talented people. It was like an actual light bulb going off when they had ideas. She wondered what his aura was like while he painted. Or what it was like when he made love... And *where* did that thought come from? She concentrated on the menu he handed her.

They ordered their food, sipped tangy margaritas and munched through two baskets of salty chips and salsa while they waited.

She laughed as they made their way back loaded with three carryout bags.

When they again stood in front of the coffee shop, he jerked his head towards the gallery. "Want to come to my place to eat?"

"Because it's so much closer to the paints?" she asked.

"I said nothing about paints." He blinked. "Sorry. You're just a great subject."

"At least I'm a great something." Okay, so hot thoughts must be put on hold since the man lived with his daughter.

Probably a good thing to go slow. Slow allowed one time to think. And thinking was good. Perhaps if she'd done more thinking in her life previously, then she might not be so torn up about what to do in her life now.

For a woman who had always just followed where fate led her, she'd questioned more in the last several months than in her entire life. *Thank you, fate.* And second-guessing was exhausting. Fate, roads, belief.

Shaking off the thoughts that never left her completely

alone, she focused back on the sexy man beside her. Instead of entering the front door of the gallery, he walked around to the side to an arched adobe gateway with a tall wooden turquoise gate. The latch clicked as he opened and held the gate for her. She strode over the flagstones laid in the ground. Here at the back, a staircase led up to the second floor.

"I bet this courtyard is beautiful later in the year," she said softly.

He grinned. "I admit, I like gardening and yes, it is. Maybe you'll see it then."

She licked her lips. Would she still be here? "Maybe I will."

The door at the top of the steps opened and Alyssa barreled down the stairs, her black heeled boots clunking with the ease and grace of youth. "Later, Dad. Don't wait up."

"Alyssa." He juggled and almost dropped one of the bags until Lake reached out and caught it. "Where are you going?"

"Dad, I'm fine. I'll be in later. *Really* later, so have fun. I've got my cell phone, feel free to call, just not too many times. I'll be with Mark."

"Mark?" He frowned.

"Howard, coffee shop. Graphic artist major. Though he's thinking of double majoring in business administration."

He shook his head. "What about—"

"He wants to talk to me about the summer semester because registration starts next week." Alyssa quickly kissed his cheek and darted around them. "You guys have fun, don't wait up and spare the speech, Dad. I'm not nine. I'd be at NYU if not for last year, and then you'd have *no* idea what I was doing."

"But Thad, aren't you guys dating?"

Alyssa laughed. "Mark and I are *talking* about school, Dad.

Jeez, it's not a date. And even if it was, Thad's..." She shrugged and walked backward towards the gate. "He's himself and I'm me and we're not *really* dating, we're just, you know, casual."

"Casual," Max said.

The whirling burst of energy all but danced out the gate. The latch clicked into the silence. Cars drove by on the street and both adults were left standing holding bags.

"Ahhh," Lake said into the baffled silence. "To be young and carefree again."

"She's never carefree." He drew in a deep breath. "And what the hell does casual mean?"

"Do you really want to know?"

His eyes held no humor as they locked on hers.

"I think it means, mind your own business."

He scoffed.

"Be thankful for times like these." She looked at the gate with thoughts of youth and fun in her head and just like that, darkness swept in.

Black fog. Alyssa walking, hurrying, thinking...

Broken images.

Fear.

Evil...

The vision wasn't clear...

Darkness trailed through the air, tentacles swirling closer and closer to Alyssa...

The images broke, scattered.

Eyes in containers.

From before.

Lake jerked and almost dropped the bag.

"Hey, you okay?" Max asked her in his deep voice.

Lake could only stand there like an idiot staring at the gate. The gate Alyssa had gone through, walked through, seemed to mock her.

Darkness still hung in the air. She shivered.

What did it mean? Did it mean anything?

"Watch out for her," she said softly.

"What?"

"Alyssa, watch her." She licked her lips. "Nothing, sorry, just...nothing."

He frowned and said, "Come on, you're cold. Let's get inside and eat."

The truth was, she was no longer hungry. For months she'd had shields in place, even as she had wanted to reconnect with herself. Yet when she lowered her shields, rarely could she...could she...*feel* or sense to any degree she used to. But not this time. This time, the feelings had all but blindsided her.

What did they mean?

She had been of no help before, not when she needed to be, not when it really mattered, when it really counted.

And only once had she had this feeling before, back in Sedona when Cora had almost died.

This darkness, an overcast sky, shrouded her senses. Was this real? Was she projecting feelings from the nightmare before?

"Hey?" His hand on her shoulder pulled her back. "Lake? You okay?"

She looked at him, then back at the gate. The feeling deep in her gut was the same—she had to do something. Maybe this was fate giving her a second chance to help, to stop the darkness she'd missed before.

She tried to smile and walked up the stairs.

Now she just had to figure out how to stop the darkness.

Chapter Three

Alyssa walked quickly down the sidewalk. Good, her dad might actually get some tonight, and if not tonight, then in the near future. Most kids freaked at the idea of parents and sex, which she thought was stupid. How the hell did the kids think they got there in the first place? Granted, she didn't dwell on it, but she'd had sex. She knew her dad. If he scored, he would be thinking about Lake, and then he'd be thinking about something other than her. Something other than what she was wearing, where she was going, if she was eating enough, worrying if she'd suddenly go off the damn deep end.

Deep end.

She shoved her hands into the pockets of her dark red pea coat. Her boots felt tight and her knee was stiff and hurting. Probably about to get colder in the next couple of days.

Something was coming.

Something bad.

The deep end.

What the hell was the deep end anyway? She'd been so close to it before, it was almost familiar ground. Like climbing the same high peak and looking just a bit further over the edge. Then a little bit further, confident she wouldn't fall.

But she could. She knew that all too well.

Hell, she'd seen more doctors, more shrinks in her short life than anyone else she knew. And that was before her mother and brother had died in the accident that almost claimed her own life.

Had it really been over a year already? She'd been in a coma for three months after that, and then rehab, coming here to live with Dad and all the rounds upon rounds of doctor appointments. Apparently time flew when she was having fun. One thing she had to give Dad, he never asked if she *saw* people that no one else saw. He never asked what her dreams were about. More importantly, he never felt the need to pick her quietness apart, piece by piece as if looking for some malfunction or disorder or something. Her father, though hovering and too worrisome, gave her much-needed space. Not like Mom.

Her latest therapy sessions had been with a grief counselor and she didn't need that woman to tell her that she was angry with her mother. That she was angry at her mother for dying in the stupid car accident, a car accident that could have been avoided if her mother had just for *once* listened to her.

They'd argued just that morning because Alyssa had been stupid enough to tell her mother she had a bad feeling about that day. She'd learned long before then to keep most of herself, of what went on inside her, to herself. But that time, that time it had been so strong. She had broken her own rule not to talk to Mom about what she "knew/saw/envisioned". Those had been terrifying words to her mother and any of them, or anything to do with them, usually resulted in a new doctor, in new meds. But Mom hadn't listened, she never listened. She'd only yelled at her to stop being dramatic.

"Mom, please, please listen—"

"Just stop, Alyssa. I can't take this anymore. Get in the damned car!"

Absently, Alyssa rubbed her inner wrists along the pocket's edge, feeling the scars that still marked the skin from a stupid night when she'd been too close to that edge, that beckoning edge, which had pulled her closer and closer until her mother had found her in the shower and called nine-one-one. That had been the summer between her sophomore and junior year. That had resulted in her parents having one hellacious fight.

Stop!

She paused, blinked and looked around.

A dark feeling crept closer and closer, all but slithering around her ankles.

She stepped back.

Angry red spears danced around her. Was she really the only person who could see them?

What if she was wrong? What if she really wasn't psychic? What if she was as crazy as her mother and the hordes of Midwestern doctors had always believed?

She wasn't crazy. She wasn't.

Belief in herself was important. She knew that, had heard that, time and again from many around here.

Belief in herself.

The darkness seemed to gather strength, to grow. To breathe. To gain power, gain color.

Red.

The bright red dimmed, swirled, but never went away. The daggers danced closer and closer to her. Almost aiming at her.

Or were they?

Calm down. Stay calm.

Her breathing slowed and chills danced wickedly on her skin.

Where the hell was this coming from? Evil energy hissed through the air and she stumbled back a step into a group of laughing college coeds.

The red daggers at the edge of the dark essence morphed together, then shot away as if disjointed, needing something...

Or someone?

She rubbed her arms.

The thick air snaked and coiled, threatening.

Who was it? She glanced around, looking, searching...

He smiled as he watched her from the shadows. Where did she think she was going?

She could feel him.

Oh yes, she could feel him. He was sure of it. From here he could see her eyes, watchful, fearful. And he'd even shielded himself, hadn't he? He thought he had. Perhaps his powers had waned more than he had thought. It wouldn't be a surprise. Not a surprise at all, not with all the meds and sicknesses rushing through his body.

Her pale face was almost ghostlike in the wash of street lights, in the neon lights that flashed from one nearby bar and grill. Tourists spilled out onto the sidewalk around her.

That should confuse things.

Confusion was good. It didn't allow one to focus on the important, on the tendril that could lead to him.

Her power hummed through the space between them, warm, dented, yet innocent at the same time, even as it was edged with darkness, layered with...so many layers and complexities.

He frowned.

Innocent and darkness in one? Warm yet... He closed his eyes... Cold at the same time.

Both?

She was unsure of herself.

He already knew that.

He knew about this one, knew she was gifted, though he had no idea she was this interesting.

A shame really. She was such a sweet girl. Sweet and nice and—

He shuddered as pain bit through his head, snaked down his spine. Nausea rolled his belly, and ice all but skittered over his skin.

Should have worn a coat or stayed inside.

But something had called to him to come out this night, to see, to *hunt*.

And now he knew.

He had hoped otherwise, but what was to be, would be, no matter what he or anyone else wanted to do.

Her darted looks, the eyes all but black from here, scanned back and forth before they zeroed in on the space where he hid.

She took one step.

Yes. Come to me, sweet.

Her black spiky hair glinted blue in the night lights as she shook her head. She froze, and jerked back.

No!

Her own silent voice screamed to him. *Run! Run!*

He smiled. It wouldn't do any good for her to run. He knew where she was, where she went. Who she was. He knew a lot about her.

He'd found his next one and the power of her alone... He trembled, the night and cold enveloping him as she turned and fled down the street.

It didn't matter. He knew where she'd run.

Maybe he'd make this one slow, build it up. If she knew she was hunted, she'd try harder to fight him—increasing her will to live.

If she wanted to live even more, then she'd fight him harder.

The charge from that alone...

If he could still get an erection, he'd have a hard-on the size a whore would be proud of.

But the illness and meds had taken a lot from him. A lot that he hated. A lot that he wanted back.

That he *would* get back with the power of the transfers, with the power he took from them.

A chuckle surprised him. This one he would enjoy. This one he was looking forward to.

She was so powerful and she had no idea.

But he did.

And he'd have her and all her unharnessed power very, very soon.

Alyssa stumbled as she turned and ran.

Run! Run! Run!

The mantra screamed in her brain.

The darkness took on shapes, shapes she couldn't make out from those around her, but she could feel them as they pressed against her, a cacophony of feelings, emotions, sounds.

Help us! Help us!

You must stop him.

He must be stopped!

He wants you—

He needs you.

He'll have you if you're not careful.

Run! Run! Run!

The voices screamed inside her head, none of them her own, all of them loud and terrifying.

She halted to get her bearings. Home, she was almost at home, but she couldn't go home.

Dad was there. With a woman.

She'd go anyway. *Home. Safety.*

She took a step across the street and then stopped. *No. No.*

Raw nerves trembled through her, her limbs weak and shaking.

What would Dad say? Her mother... No. Dad wasn't like that, he'd listen.

Sorry to rain on your date, but I had a vision.

A vision? Something else?

Pressure built within her.

She could feel it—them—whatever, pushing against her shields. Shields she'd constructed over the years to stop the voices, to stop the visions, to stop the knowing.

It wasn't real.

"It's not real. It's not real. It's not real."

A hand on her shoulder ripped a scream from her throat even as a voice asked, "Alyssa?"

She whirled, and stared into bright blue eyes.

The trembling wouldn't stop.

"Hey. Hey, Alyssa. What the hell?"

"Mark. Mark." She stood there, just staring at him, her thoughts ragged and scattered, unfocused.

He looked from her to behind her, up and down the street. His tall frame towered over her and she didn't know if she should run home and to hell with her father's woman-date-whatever, or if she should...

"Come inside. Okay?" Mark took her arm and guided her into the coffee shop he ran at night for his parents.

Without a word, she let him lead her to the bar that guarded the side of the coffee shop. Patrons sat at tables, and a few glanced at them as he walked her to the last stool.

"Here, sit down, now."

"Hey, buddy, we'd like to pay here," said a man standing at the head of the bar, by the register.

"Just a minute."

The man huffed and muttered something about service to the woman with him.

Warmth from the coffee shop hugged its arms around her, pulled her back, slowly at first, then seemed to jerk her back to where she was. To the here and now. Not to that other space somewhere between worlds that only she seemed to be aware of.

Maybe she really was freaking nuts.

Noise clattered against her eardrums. The soft indie rock that played from the speakers beat slowly on the air, mixing with the clunk of mugs on the glass tables, laughing with voices and murmurs of the customers. Heady coffee fragrances melded together and jolted her as surely as if she'd had a shot of espresso.

Alyssa took a deep breath and steadied herself.

"Better?" Mark asked.

She could only nod her head.

For a moment, his blue eyes studied her before he frowned, then walked behind and down the bar to the impatient customer still muttering to the woman with him.

When they paid, the old fashioned register trilling out a bell as the drawer opened, she took another breath.

Mark turned and filled a white mug, then plopped it in front of her with a narrowed look that might as well have commanded, "Drink it."

Alyssa tried to smile and knew she failed, but cupped the mug in her palms in an attempt to warm herself.

She focused on the things around her, but wasn't able to let it all in.

Instead she focused on Mark. Watched him move from the coffee dispensers to the glass-domed cake displays to the cookie jars.

His hands were long-fingered, the wrists sinewy. She knew from this past summer that his arms were muscled, as were his legs. He sometimes rode bikes with her dad in the mornings. Other mornings he jogged and she knew he liked to snowboard.

He was her friend and she was sort of seeing his brother, Thad.

Sort of. Or not. She still wasn't certain and to be honest, wasn't really concerned about it. She and Thad didn't really have a "relationship", but she had a feeling that if she started to flirt with Mark, he'd have an issue with it.

Mark was the quietest of the three boys, she'd learned. He

often reminded her of her father with his solemn glances, studying intently as if trying to figure out the workings of things, the very essence of whatever he perused.

As far as she knew, he still hadn't decided what he wanted to be, what he wanted to do. He was twenty-two, already had a bachelor's in criminal justice but was taking computer graphics and business courses just now. His older brother, Thad, was working on a master's in education while subbing at local schools in his off time.

Alyssa wondered what the differences were between them all. She had very little to do with the youngest brother, Kevin, who was her own age, but he was...he was...

Scattered.

Like Mark, Kevin wasn't certain what he wanted to do and had only taken a course or two at the local community college, but unlike Mark, he had no direction. Kevin seemed perfectly happy to run the ski lifts at the resort a few miles up the road and work with the forest service through the summer. She'd often figured he was taking the courses to appease his family.

Would Timmy have been like Mark? Or Kevin? Probably Kevin. Her brother had hidden parts of himself from their mother. He had been wiser than her and, God, she missed him.

Taking a deep breath, she shook off the morose thoughts.

"Thad should be here soon," Mark said as he wiped the counter in front of her.

She frowned before she could stop herself. "Mark, a couple of kisses does not a relationship make."

He only looked at her.

"Please, I know your brother and we're not really seeing each other. I mean, we went out a few times. He's cool. I like him, but can you really see either of us together, seriously?"

For a moment he said nothing, then he shrugged. "I don't know, if you wanted to, both of you, you would be."

An education major. She would bet Thad would never *get* her. She stared at the coffee in the mug and swirled it with a swizzle stick. No one would *ever* get her. And Thad was too analytical, too into this world and proper this and proper way of that to think out of the box.

They were not right for each other, but he was fun and a nice guy. For her, dates had always seemed more like hanging with a friend, and seemed to be missing...something.

"I like your brother, he'll always be a great friend and trust me, he feels the same for me."

A hand at the base of her neck squeezed lightly. "I do?"

She jumped and pulled into herself, leaned to the side so that his hand fell from her neck. She hadn't even felt him come upon her.

God, what was wrong with her?

Her hands shook as she brought the mug to her lips.

"You okay?" Thad asked, sitting down on the stool beside her.

She didn't miss the look he shared with his brother. The *what's-going-on* look.

"Why does everyone keep asking me that?" she muttered, anger rising within her. What the hell was she supposed to tell them? *No, I'm not okay, I see things, you know, daggers, red fog, evil. You? How's your evening going? Oh and by the way, your aura is a bit off.* Shaking her head, she threw the thoughts away and glared at Thad.

"What are you doing here?"

One blond brow rose. "My parents own the joint."

Idiot.

She glanced at Mark, but he held her stare with a narrow gaze and then went to fill an order.

Alyssa set her mug down. "I'm fine. I just want—" No, want was the wrong word. "I *need* to be alone." To figure things out. How the hell was she supposed to deal with all this when she'd fought it all her life?

"Well, you don't look fine, you're pale as the cream and your eyes are sunken dark orbs."

A smile surprised her. "And on the moonlit waters dreamed…" she muttered.

"What?"

Thad, like Mark, was handsome with the golden Adonis good looks, the straight features, almost aristocratic, but a bit too edged to be that smooth. A couple days' worth of stubble dusted his jawline. The family's bright blue eyes had not skipped him and now they looked confused.

"Dark orbs, pale as cream?" She wagged a finger at him. "You're teaching poetry again aren't you?"

"I—well—that's not the point." He turned so that he faced her fully. "You are very complicated, Alyssa Gray."

"Tell me something I don't know, Thaddeus Howard."

For one long minute he studied her. "I don't know that there isn't much you don't know. You've got great eyes, but you know that too."

She grinned, "Knowing it and hearing it again are two different things. Women love compliments, don't you know?" She snapped her fingers. "You forgot, didn't you. Please don't give the next girl the sunken-eyed-dark-orbs. It's bad. No wonder you're not married yet."

He huffed and sat back. "I beg your pardon. I've no intention of getting married, thank you very much. If and when

I do, I assure you, I'll know what I'm doing."

Mark walked up and laughed. "Uh-huh. Remember to compliment the woman's eyes so she'll be so distracted she'll accept. Otherwise Mom might never get her wedding."

Thad reached across the bar and playfully shoved his brother back a few steps. "I'm working here."

"Is that what you were doing? And here I thought you were talking." Mark looked at Alyssa. "You're work now. Isn't that nice? Work has such lovely eyes."

She laughed.

Her laugh warmed him. Alyssa's smiling face, her eyes currently free of phantoms, unfurled the fist that had squeezed his heart when he'd seen her standing out on the sidewalk, ashen-faced and wide-eyed.

Alyssa. She called to him, had since the first time he'd seen her over a year ago limping carefully into her father's gallery. She'd been a silent ghost who had hidden in the gallery for months before venturing out.

Slowly, like a chrysalis, she was morphing into a strong woman. He could feel that around her, this...charisma.

He grinned back at her and rolled his eyes at Thad. Thad, what a stupid idiot. The guy could have had her, but maybe she hadn't wanted him. God knew Thad had plenty of girls at the college, and he'd have more when he transferred to the University of New Mexico at Santa Fe or New Mexico State in Las Cruses. Mark had the feeling that Miss Gray wasn't the long distance type. But as she just pointed out, she wasn't really Thad's type either.

He tilted his head and watched as she punched Thad in the arm.

She was a butterfly. The shy girl still lurked, still darted back into hiding from time to time, but mostly, here she sat. Brash, up front and strangely vulnerable.

And she rarely looked at him twice.

Hell, tonight he'd called her to tell her about her dad and Lake in hopes of just talking to her. Surprised the hell out of him when she'd said she would use him as an excuse to get out of the house. They'd talk about college.

College.

"You could always come with me, Alyssa," Thad said, jerking Mark out of his musings.

"What? With you? To college, where?"

"Wherever," Thad answered, giving her the famous Howard smile, sure to get a woman to go along with whatever they wanted.

Mark sure as hell didn't want her going along with Thad and his plans.

Alyssa only laughed. "Uh-huh. I'd probably kill you in a few weeks." She waved her hand towards the outside. "Besides, I like it here."

"In Taos?" Thad's bafflement was clear. His well-known hatred of the mountain town was a mystery to them all.

"Big bro here wants big city," Mark said, wiping glasses and mugs dry before he set them on the bar. "Big city, big lights."

"Big crime," she finished and shuddered, then took a drink of her coffee. "Thanks, but no thanks. Big cities are not for me. Been there, done that. I don't want any more of it. Taos maybe...maybe..." Her eyes stared past Mark to focus on the wall behind him.

In the gray-blue depths he saw again dark shadows before she blinked.

"Maybe what? A high-dollar cowboy town? Please, it's a tourist trap," Thad muttered and stood, walking behind the bar.

Mark could see the signs of aggravation in his brother's tense lips and narrowed eyes. He knew the normal tirade was coming. Nothing here, nowhere to go, unless you wanted to be in real estate or be a shop owner or...

Alyssa tilted her head. The dim lights glinted softly in her short dark hair, which didn't seem so spiky now, but lay in soft curls, probably because she kept running a hand through it—like she did now.

He loved her hands. The way the long fingers drummed, the way he could see the tendons and bones, the movement of knuckles. He had a thing for hands—not sure what—but he noticed hands and eyes on people and in art. Both were exceptional in Alyssa's case.

She waved a hand in his direction. "He'll never get it, will he?"

Mark grinned and shook his head.

Thad opened his mouth and she held her hand palm out. "Nope. I don't want to hear all the great city accolades. I don't care about living in the big city, and be serious, Thad, you're so not a one-woman man."

"And you're a one-man woman?"

She thought about it. Her pursed lips—damned fine lips, too—curved into a smile. The bottom was plumper than the top so that she almost always appeared to be pouting. "I could be."

"If the right guy came along?" Thad served himself a cup of coffee. The bar had dwindled down to the nighttime regulars scattered at three different tables.

Mark didn't miss her glance at him. "Something like that." Then she shrugged, one shouldered, and grinned. "But I seriously doubt there's a man alive who would put up with me and all my...eccentricities."

"You might be surprised," both he and his brother said at the same moment.

Chapter Four

Lake stared at the art around the studio. "So this is where the madness begins?" She turned to him. The night-shadowed windows framed her. "Or rather where it is created, I suppose."

"What?" Max set the food containers on the scarred, paint-splattered table top.

His overhead lights caught the different shades of blonde and red in her hair as she tilted her head. "Well, who knows where the madness began."

He frowned. "What madness?"

Madness? Was she talking about Alyssa? An old defense licked his ire.

Her hands fluttered and waved at the half-finished canvases he would probably never display because most of them still lacked something. "The creative madness. Art in all its various forms." She shrugged and trailed a long nail down the frameless canvas of a moonlit landscape.

He sighed and closed his eyes. Damn his ex-wife. One should never speak ill of the dead, but the fact was she had done a number not only on him, but worse, also on his daughter. Madness. He could all but hear that woman's voice yelling about the madness in his family and how she wouldn't allow it to affect Alyssa, how she'd do *anything* in her power to keep Alyssa normal.

Max shook off the thoughts and opened the containers. Spicy steam wafted in the air. He grabbed a couple of plastic utensils out of one of the drawers.

From the corner of his eye, he noticed Lake strolling along, stopping at this or that painting or photograph, items by locals he had yet to display. This was the catch-all art storage room, where he usually ate when working instead of in his own kitchen.

He had nothing to drink. Well, there was wine, but to be honest, he didn't care for wine with spicy Mexican food. It was one of the only times he really wanted a beer, and if he was lucky, he'd still have a few in the fridge.

She, however, looked like she was a wine woman.

And this was why he didn't date, especially hot-as-hell Viking goddesses with long red hair and wicked dark green eyes.

"Bad shape here, bud," he muttered to himself.

"Did you say something?" she asked him.

"Oh." Max scratched his goatee and smiled. "I was just wondering what I had for us to drink. Wine, if you want some."

"What are you having?" Her gaze was direct and unwavering, reminding him of his daughter for some unknown reason.

"Uh—beer. I think there are a couple of Dos Equis in the fridge. Um, in the kitchen."

She smiled, her full lips tugging his attention to her mouth and away from what he'd like to drink, or at least from the beer.

"That's fine."

He blinked. "What?"

Her brows rose.

"Oh, right. Right. Beer. Be right back." He closed the studio door, then leaned back against the hallway's wall. "Idiot. Way to go, ace." He thunked his head on the wall.

At this rate he'd never get her in bed. Not that that was the only reason he was with her. She was interesting, very interesting, in fact. The image of her with his daughter flashed in his mind, the way she'd taken it all in stride. Didn't even so much as blink. In fact, with her line of work, she wholeheartedly believed in auras and visions and "just knowing", as his daughter would say. Then again, with her new age shop, or whatever she had, maybe it was all just part of business. He'd like to not think so. Auras...

Get it together.

Beer. She'd think he was a lost case if he didn't actually get the beer in there before the food got cold.

"Bad, bad shape," he said yet again as he made his way to the door at the end of the hallway, which led to the apartment. He grabbed four beers and hurried back to the studio.

"So," she said as he popped the tops off two bottles and set them on the table. "You do your own stuff, but you exhibit very little of it downstairs, at least that I've seen. You show your own photographs, but most of the sculptures and paintings or jewelry are by someone else." She waved a hand towards canvases stacked against the wall. "Yet here are more canvases than I care to count and you've painted them all."

"Not all of them." He slid a glance to the far corner where Alyssa liked to work sometimes.

She followed his gaze. "No, probably not all."

They sat down. "Do you ever display your own paintings?"

He grinned. "Not good enough."

She laughed, a full throaty sound that reminded him of silk in moonlight. He shifted in his chair.

"Not good enough? Please. Art, no matter the form, is totally subjective. In several years people wonder why they purchased most things adorning their walls and shelves they claim was or is art. And then they go out and buy more that calls to them at that time."

"And things have to call to you?"

She picked up her fork and scooped up Southwest rice. "Of course. If something didn't call to you, then why do it? Or in art's case, purchase it? It wouldn't be right."

He picked up his own fork and started to eat. "So you believe in callings, fate..." He stopped, then shrugged. "Auras."

"I thought we'd already been over this."

"Humor me, please, and don't take offense at a question."

Those wicked green eyes narrowed just at the corners. "That would depend on the question, wouldn't it?"

"And who's asking it, or maybe why."

"True."

Her eyes closed on a bite of chile relleno. "This is really, really good. I love these. They should be savored, explored and thoroughly enjoyed."

My thoughts exactly. She was gorgeous, there was simply no other word for it. Outer beauty, yes, she had that, but there was an inner fire, an inner life that...called to him. He grinned and forked another bite into his mouth.

"The question?" she probed.

"Your beliefs, your shop, is it all..." He would offend her, but hell, he was a guy, just like any other. "Is it all...?"

"Is it all...?" She leaned up on her elbows, that lovely cleavage pressing against the dress.

He jerked his gaze away from her breasts and to her face. "Is it real?"

A furrow creased the skin between her brows. "Is it real? As in?"

He sighed and laid his fork aside. "As in, is it just part of the job, nine to five? Or is it *who* you really are?"

Those eyes continued to stare at him, the pupils dilating softly for several long moments before she blinked, drew a deep breath and said, "And you ask why?"

He grinned. "Well, some people create...personas, if you will, for their businesses. While at home, they have another face, and with those they see at the club, maybe another facet. Yet none make the whole. Ya know? Everyone has facets. I get that. I like..." He curled his fingers into the air. "I like raw, real, no matter the setting."

She merely stared at him.

"I'm not great at explanations. The thing is, I like you. I've watched you over at the coffee shop watching me, and tried to figure out how to ask you out."

"While I wondered if I could work up the nerve to ask you out," she said, her voice slow and easy.

He grinned. "Really?"

She smiled back.

"The point is that I've noticed you, not sure what or why at first, but I did. I haven't in a long while. Noticed a woman, that is. But something about you has intrigued me since the moment I first saw you ordering a cup of coffee at the café."

Her throaty laugh danced out again and her hand covered his on the table.

"Same goes. There was a time I was too..." Those plump lips pursed. "Easy with my affections and then I became very guarded, and still am guarded. You're the first man I've noticed in a while."

Okay, so they were on the same footing there, good. "Good. But with your talk of auras and knowing and stuff, I need to know you believe it, really, *really* believe it, or if it's just promotion for business."

She licked her lips. "Why?"

"My daughter," he said simply. "Alyssa is very..."

"Fragile," she finished for him.

Max stared at her a moment and thought maybe, just maybe this woman understood. He picked up his fork, then set it down and took a drink, the taste of his beer bright and sharp on his tongue.

"Yes, yes she is. So please understand that I'm not trying to offend you or anything but if you don't really believe in all that stuff, please don't bring it up around Alyssa. If talking about auras and fate and 'something calling to you' is just—"

"Shoptalk?" she asked before taking another bite.

"Yeah." He nodded. "Yeah, shoptalk."

"Just a face, or rather a mask to put on when it suits me?" She smiled. "A, what did you call it? Promotion. A promotional angle to drum up business?"

Her tone had quieted, he heard the edge to it, but damn it this was too important to set aside. "Yes. For lack of a better analogy. Masks is a great one, actually."

She laid her fork back down and laced her fingers beneath her chin. "Max. I don't lie. Or at least I try never to lie. Lying about my weight or dress size is a given."

He grinned.

"If you knew me at all, you would know that under normal circumstances, that question would not only offend me—" Her eyes flashed as she continued, "But *really* piss me off."

"I—"

"However, I understand where you're coming from—parental concern. So, to answer your question, no, it's not just shoptalk or a mask I put on for promotion's sake to drum up business. What I do, I believe in. If that bothers you, fine. I don't really care." She stared at him a moment more before she took a long drink of her beer.

He sighed. "Look. It doesn't bother me. It's just..." He raked a hand through his hair. "She's been through enough and I don't think for a moment you'd intentionally hurt my daughter, but—"

"How?"

He blinked. "How what?"

"How do you know that? That I wouldn't intentionally hurt her?"

He frowned and shrugged. "You just wouldn't."

Lake leaned forward. "Yes, you're right. No, I would never intentionally hurt her because I get the distinct feeling that girl has been through more than enough. But what I want to know is how do *you* just know this?"

"I don't know, I just do, okay?"

"And you asked me if I wore masks," she muttered before resuming her meal.

They both ate in silence for a while. His anxiety, which had plagued him all day, turned in a new direction. He'd just ruined his chance with seeing more of this fascinating woman and...

"So, you still want me to model for you?"

He paused, the bite of spinach enchilada halfway to his mouth. "Um, do you still want to?"

She grinned. "I asked you first."

His gaze ran over her, over that perfectly Renaissance face, not exactly breathtaking, not subtle, but something in between, something classic and intriguing all the same. Maybe it was the eyes, that dark green, or the fact her lips had him thinking things he was way better off not even contemplating. Or maybe it was the whole thing put together. A cross between some Irish pagan deity and a wild Viking lover.

"Yes."

That single syllable, dark and promising, slid over her like a long-awaited caress.

What the hell?

Lake scooped up more rice for the lack anything better to do and shoved it into her mouth.

The man could make her hot and cold and hot again, and her nerves were strung tighter than they'd been in a long damn time.

Though she'd really, really missed this feeling, she'd be damned if the first man who jump-started her libido could sack her that easily.

So she'd take a bit of time to reflect and question and assess.

And then jump his bones.

Very, very sad, with a capital *S*.

She'd have to figure out what the hell she wanted.

Him.

"You game?" he asked, in that same dark tone of voice.

She swallowed and almost choked. "For?" she wheezed out, grabbing her beer.

He smiled, a one-sided grin that lifted to a full-fledged smile before a laugh rumbled out.

"You know what I think?" He leaned up onto the tabletop,

his hands stacked on top of each other.

"You're gonna tell me, right? Because I hate to be kept in suspense."

His eyes narrowed fractionally. "Oh, but some suspense is good."

She nodded. "True. Some suspense is."

"The kind that leads to greater things." He wiggled his brows.

"Sex." There, she said it.

He sat back. "Now you've ruined it. We were doing so good dancing around the issue."

She merely looked at him. "We were? I thought it was more a stumbling two-step."

He frowned. "Nope. We were doing a damn fine tango."

"A fine tango?" Lake couldn't contain the chuckle. "Honey, you'll know a damn fine tango after the fact."

For a moment, he said nothing, then the corners of his eyes creased ever so slightly. "Hmmm."

She waited, but he didn't expound. "Okay, I give, what does hmmm mean?"

"Just thinking."

"Given. Of?"

"Of you. Of me. Of us. Together. Naked." His eyes never wavered from hers. "In here, with the paints. Or without. Down the hall in my bed."

"Or, since you have a daughter, maybe across the street in my bed?"

He finally blinked, and downed a drink of beer, his Adam's apple bobbing. "True. Your bed across the street."

Neither said anything for a bit.

"But—" he started.

"Not tonight," she finished.

"No, not tonight." He stood, walked to her and ran a finger over her shoulder, up her neck to trace her jaw. "Most definitely not tonight."

"Because," she whispered, "that would ruin—"

Max leaned down and she caught the scent of him yet again. "—the suspense." His breath was warm and taunting like Satan's temptation.

She sighed. Then almost jumped out of her skin as his lips nuzzled her neck.

"Relax," he said softly.

"So-sorry," she mumbled, as he kissed the side of her neck.

"For what?" One hand lifted her hair from her neck before he placed a kiss just there at her nape. Goose bumps shivered down her spine.

What had he asked? Oh yeah. "Been awhile. I'm a bit—"

"Jumpy?"

His lips were soft, yet firm, hot and inviting. She wanted them on her mouth.

"Yeah," she agreed, turning her head to his. "Yeah." Then his mouth fluttered closer and closer.

His eyes met hers. "I won't hurt you."

"Shut up."

His lips settled on hers with a passion she had glimpsed in him, in his work, in his art, in the very air around him. Perfectly checked usually, it simmered just under the surface. Energy hummed along her skin, wrapped around her as his lips pressed against hers.

To hell with it. Turning more in her chair, she cupped his

face and kissed him back.

It was as if months of self-doubt washed away to clear a brilliant path.

And that path led to Max.

The man could kiss.

Lake closed her eyes, lost herself in the pleasant, welcoming charge of being wanted. Bright lights shimmered just at the edge of her vision behind her eyelids, but she held them at bay.

Suspense.

His tongue traced her lips and she shuddered, opening her mouth to him.

Max's hands cupped her jaw, his fingers trailing into her hair as those feelings simmered stronger.

She could...she could...*feel him*. Not his physical want of her, but his desire, that elusive feeling. She could sense it, read it, so much so, she could all but taste the heady scent in the back of her mouth.

His tongue danced and dueled with hers.

Suspense, caution.

She slowly pulled back, even as his fingers momentarily gripped her head as if he didn't want her to go. Then he relaxed his hold on her and she sat back, staring into those slate gray eyes, tumultuous just now.

"We shouldn't rush it."

Those eyes stared into hers, reached into her very soul as if trying to see what was completely inside her.

Finally he said softly, "No, we shouldn't rush it. That would be a damn shame."

Then he straightened and gathered up the used containers before dumping them into the trash. He moved like a cat. Not a slick alley cat. No, he was more like a tamed...jaguar, she decided. Smooth and graceful, but just there under the edge lurked a danger.

And that was what she needed to understand first.

"I better be going," she said, standing up. "Thanks for dinner."

His smile reached his eyes. Desire still thrummed off him and battered against her, but she let it go. For now.

"You're welcome. I haven't enjoyed an evening this much in a long time."

"Me either," she agreed. Then realized how true that was. "Me either."

His head tilted to the side and the lights shot silver off the gray at his temples, and his eyes studied her again in that intense way of his.

Life father like daughter, she thought.

"I have a feeling you're being honest about that." Then he shifted, his muscles rippling under the dark purple shirt, slick and looking damn good on him. "Which sounds odd, I'm sure."

She laughed. "Odd is as odd does, and no, it doesn't. It sounds honest. Honesty is always, always preferred."

"Same goes," he added with a slight tilt of his head.

For a moment, they stared at each other. "Well, I better be going."

Motioning to the door, he said, "I'll walk you home."

"A desirable man and he's a gentleman too. Wow, will wonders never cease," she quipped.

He halted and grabbed his jacket. "He really did a number on you, didn't he?"

She met his gaze before looking down at the scuffed wooden floor. Then she plastered a smile on her face. Desire was one thing, indulging her darkest memories was not. "Suspense, remember?" She waved a hand at him. "Don't worry about walking me home. I can make it across the street."

He took a deep breath as if he was about to argue. "Fine, but I'll walk you out."

They made their way out through the hall entryway, out onto the landing and down the outside steps.

"Again, thanks for dinner. I had a great time," she said when they reached the gate.

"Me too. Do it again?"

"Definitely."

"When?"

"Whenever."

"Tomorrow morning. Breakfast."

She did laugh then, a full-throated belly laugh. "I do *not* get up at the crack of dawn like some people. I like my beauty sleep, not sweating at daybreak. I'll walk. Upon occasion, I'll ride a bike. Yoga is good. I'm not into the whole mile-or-more runs, bike rides or triathlons."

He leaned against the gate. "You get up between seven and eight. Unless you haven't slept well, then it's earlier. Then you shower and get ready before heading downstairs to have a coffee, and every two or three days a muffin with said coffee on the veranda. Unless of course, it's raining, then you like the table at the front window." He tilted his head closer to her. "I'm an artist. I notice things."

"When do the Overtons get up?" she asked, surprised he knew so much of her habits.

"The who?"

"The other renters. So it's just me you're spying on?"

"Just you. And I'm not spying. I'm observing."

She patted his arm, smiled and leaned up to kiss his cheek. "Tomorrow morning."

"Eight o'clock?"

"Eight o'clock. Sounds good."

"Until then."

She walked through the gate, stopped at the curb to let the traffic go by. Damned tourists.

"Be careful," she heard him say.

She didn't look back until she had walked across the street. He still stood there, at the gate, a half grin on his face that didn't quite reach his eyes. Maybe the man had his own thinking to do.

Then he gave her a little salute and closed the gate. She looked through the window of the coffee shop and thought about going in, but decided to head on up to her room instead. A customer shifted and she saw two of the sons behind the bar washing and drying coffee mugs. Alyssa sat laughing at the counter.

Alyssa.

From here, the girl's aura shimmered brighter than it had in a long time. Really shimmered, so many layers, the colors all mixed into a kaleidoscope of rainbows. Which wasn't unusual. Most people had different colors or shades of colors in their auras, even as one was dominant. It all depended on the person and their experiences.

But Alyssa's was literally all the colors, layered and interwoven.

Chills slithered down Lake's spine and she rubbed her arms.

"That girl needs guidance, or protection." What had made hers shimmer from dull muted colors to this bright?

Then Lake looked closer.

The aura was undoubtedly brighter, more pronounced, but, she saw something else.

Ice skittered over her skin. Terror fluttered in her heart.

Jagged scars ripped along the edges of Alyssa's aura. New scars. These were clear, colorless breaks in the aura.

Lake stepped closer, focusing.

Only one thing caused that.

Draining. Being around something or someone that drained a person's energy.

The scars were scattered, rough gouges that the surrounding colors seemed to slowly fill. Slowly healing themselves.

Lake had never seen anything like it.

She blinked and shook her head, trying to focus. How long had she been zoning? Alyssa now sat alone at the counter, the boys gone.

How long had she been standing here staring?

She knew she could lose time reading, trying to understand. She'd done it before. And this powerful girl— someone bumped into her.

"Excuse me," the voice said.

And she knew.

Don't turn around.

Don't turn around.

Darkness floated around her, enveloped her, reaching past her towards...

Lake stared into the coffee shop and just like that, Alyssa's head jerked up and her face paled. Then she shoved off the chair and strode towards the door.

No. No! Stay inside. She had to stay inside.

Lake all but stumbled into the door and caught Alyssa, who didn't even seem to see her.

"Hi, Alyssa," Lake said, her hand firm on the girl's arm.

Alyssa tried to jerk away.

"No," Lake said softly to her. "He's strong, whoever the bastard is. Let him go. He's...he's..."

"Dark," the young woman finished, then relaxed as a shudder danced through her small frame. Her eyes still stared out into the night. "Dark and...and..."

"Evil."

Alyssa finally turned to Lake, her eyes glazed and haunted. "He is. Very evil. I sensed him before."

Then she blinked, looked around and jerked her arm free. "I want to go home. I just want to go home."

"I'll walk you."

"I can walk myself," the young woman said, with the slight belligerence youth seemed to have stamped on itself.

"You can, yes, I'm sure, but I wanted to ask you something." Lake again took Alyssa's arm as they walked back across the street. Both of them looked up the street into the night-cloaked shadows.

Where was he?

"Can we get together sometime?" Lake asked, following pure instinct for the first time since the nightmare months ago.

"Why?" Alyssa asked. Something on the young woman tinkled, some piece of bling.

"Because, it's important."

They stood outside the gate. Lake knew what to look for and wasn't surprised to see Alyssa's pupils dilate ever so slightly as the young woman studied her. Then she shook her head as if shaking off the remnants of their experience. "Yeah, it's probably the smart thing to do. When?"

"Tomorrow? I'm having breakfast with your dad at eight, why don't you join us? Or me? Afterwards? Whatever."

Alyssa tilted her head, just like her father, and then grinned. "You're definitely different. Dad might have other plans for breakfast."

True, he might. "This is important. Either at breakfast or I'll meet you later."

"You don't think I'm weird? Strange?"

Lake only laughed. "Get inside so I know you're safe. I'll see you in the morning."

She watched the girl walk up the stairs, watched her go into the door. Finally, Lake turned and hurried across the street.

What the hell had she landed herself in?

Chapter Five

Sunlight, dull and gray, filtered the morning light. The snow so many had felt and smelled on the air had settled on the tip of Taos Mountain, which would undoubtedly make the skiers happy.

Max rolled his shoulders, realizing he hadn't slept well. Not that he'd dreamed, at least not that he remembered. He'd thought of Lake. He'd thought of Alyssa, and somewhere in his mind the two had entangled and had left him worried and anxious.

He could still see the way Lake had looked at the gate last night after Alyssa had walked through it, warning him to watch out for her.

Irritation slithered through him as he finished shaving. Cold outside air blew fresh through the cracked window. He hated stuffy air and, though it was cold, it wasn't that cold. Max breathed deep and tried again to figure out what worried him about...about...what?

Was it that Alyssa was more at peace lately than she had been in a long time? That she was no longer worried—or quite so worried—that she was weird and different? Actually, she'd probably always be weird and different by some people's standards, but she was a tad more mainstream than she had been. Taos was eclectic enough she'd always fit in here.

They rarely talked about her gift, and he blamed himself and her mother for that. He hadn't been there when he needed to protect her. But that was all in the past. He was here now and he'd help her any way he could.

So why did it bother him so much that a woman he rather liked, or was attracted to and interested in, didn't bat an eyelash at his daughter? Had even complimented her on her gifts and had mentioned how very gifted she was?

It wasn't that he didn't believe in his daughter or Lake's acceptance, wasn't that he did, either. He was open enough to know that not everything could be crammed into a neat textbook that psychiatrists and other docs or people could study. Some things simply *were*. He sometimes had an idea, a gut instinct of what to do or not do, and it rarely steered him wrong. His mother and grandmother had both simply *known* things. No one questioned them on it. His family believed in the power of dreams, how sometimes messages weren't left on answering machines or written to be plainly read, but left in that strange realm between awake and asleep.

He didn't doubt Alyssa, not really. But sometimes she liked to shock just for shock's sake, and he had no idea if she was using her gift or just being obnoxious. Sometimes he could tell the difference. Sometimes not.

Like last night. She'd come in, pale, her eyes wide with phantoms dancing in their depths. She'd awakened like that sometimes as a child, after a dream about something that inevitably happened or came true—like knowing where the little missing boy from their neighborhood had been. After the accident she'd awakened the first few months with that look of fear on her face, her eyes darker than normal.

The dreams, the knowing, all had been too much for his ex. She'd frowned upon anything outside of what she considered normal. Like Alyssa's sensitivities, his ex had often seen him as abnormal. He remembered the fights and he remembered the day he left, moving here to Taos, believing his children were in better hands with their mother.

Stupid. So foolishly stupid.

The razor nicked his chin.

"Shit."

And that was what thinking about his ex always got him, bloodshed—and the woman was dead, for the love of God.

One should never think ill of the dead, but the truth was, he never should have left his kids with her, and he was only just coming to accept the truth of that.

A soft knock on his bedroom door pulled his attention back to the here and now.

"Dad?" Alyssa's voice wafted out from his room.

"Just a sec!" He quickly dressed, wiped his bleeding chin with the back of his hand and sighed. Several moments later, he opened the door. She was dressed in normal clothes, jeans and a tie-dyed pullover—thank whatever drove teenagers to pick their attire. Her eyes widened and she rubbed her arms.

"I'm going with you."

He blinked. "I'm sorry?"

"To breakfast." She checked her black braided leather watch, the face square, with skulls as the minute and hour hands. "We're going to be late if you don't hurry. For crying out loud, Dad, it's just breakfast." She frowned, leaned up and wiped his chin. "You weren't paying attention."

"You're going? To breakfast? With me?"

Her brows rose. "Yes. Yes. Yes. And Lake. She invited me last night. She wants to talk over something with me."

"What?" he asked. It was his turn to frown. "Talk over what?" Liking a woman was one thing, but if she thought she could use his daughter to get close to him, or use Alyssa for anything, *anything* else, she was sorely mistaken. "When?" He snapped, walking to his dresser to grab a pair of socks.

"Last night after I left the coffee shop."

Last night when Alyssa came in looking lost and alone and too quiet for his peace of mind. Of course she hadn't said anything, and had turned the conversation neatly around so quickly he'd only realized it later.

"Why did she talk to you last night?" he asked, watching her carefully, anger simmering in him. He'd actually liked the woman, but his daughter was not the way to win him over, damn it. He thought they had covered this last night. He'd been down this road before.

Dating was a pain in the ass.

She tapped the door frame and only said, "Hurry up. I don't want to be late and I'm in *dire* need of caffeine, Father dear." She batted her long-lashed eyes at him and darted down the hallway.

"Dammit." He quickly jerked on his shoes and pulled a lightweight jacket out of the closet. As he strode down the hall to the living room, he asked again, "Why, Alyssa?"

Her eyes went blank. "I don't want to talk about it."

His defenses slammed up. "I think perhaps Miss Lake and I should have a chat."

She rolled her eyes and the anger simmered more. "Dad, come on. I'm not a child."

He strode to her. "You are *my* child. I don't care how damned old you are. I watched you lying in a hospital bed so close to death I couldn't...I couldn't... Your brother was..." He took a deep breath. "You may be nineteen-going-on-forty and I know in the past, I wasn't there like I should have been, but you are still *mine* to protect. And if she thinks..."

"She helped me," Alyssa said softly, her fingers fidgeting.

He fisted his hands on his hips. "With?"

Her drawn-out sigh was full of teenage angst. "Stuff. Can we eat now? I promise you can rip into her if I can watch." She turned and her eyes flashed. "Because I can tell you, Lake will rip right back. She's nice, she...she..."

"What?" he asked, shutting the door behind them before following her down the outer hallway to the outside door. "She's what, Alyssa? We're not going until you answer me."

Alyssa whirled, hurt, anger and something else flashing in her eyes. "She understands, Dad! She understands what it's...what it's... She understands what's *in* me. She understands!"

"Alyssa," he tried calmly, "we just met this woman."

She turned, jerked the outside door open and flew down the steps. Nineteen. Had he been this torn up inside at nineteen? Probably not.

God, Dad was *so* difficult. The man knew nothing. Not a damned thing! Alyssa didn't wait for him. Instead she hurried across the street, narrowly missing a cyclist who'd decided to use the sidewalk as his private path.

"Watch it!" she yelled. "There's a road!" She slammed into the coffee shop.

She looked around and then quickly made her way to the back, but she saw no Lake sitting at any of the tables. What the hell was with adults? Especially laid-back adults like her father and apparently Lake?

"You look happy this morning," Mark said beside her.

She hadn't even noticed him. There was a first time for everything, she supposed. "Lake?"

Mark raised one blond brow. "Haven't seen her. Oh wait, yeah. Out on the front patio." He jerked his head to the front of the store. "You went right past her."

She turned and saw her dad standing there talking to Lake, who sported shades, a jacket and a bright purple scarf and sat at a table beneath a green umbrella.

"That woman likes purple," Mark muttered.

Her father fisted his hands on his hips. Great. She knew that look on his face, that set, carved look. The "don't-push-it" face.

"What's steamed him?" Mark asked.

Alyssa took a deep breath and smelled Mark's cologne, the mixture of sweetness and spice that somehow fit him. "Oh, someone might have upset me or something. He's just so—so—so... Arg! I'm not a little kid." She looked at Mark out of the corner of her eye. His hair was longer on top, so that he was always raking it back off his forehead. Those bright blue eyes of his studied her.

"What?" she asked.

"You look..."

She cocked a brow and planted her own fist on her hip.

"Nice. You look really nice."

She'd rolled out of bed and pulled on the jeans she wore yesterday and a tie-dyed blue-green tee shirt with a jacket. She frowned. "Thank you."

He smiled. "Why do compliments always throw you, make you pause?"

She thought about it for a minute then shrugged. "I don't know."

"I'll have to keep at them then." They both watched the little scene unfold outside, Lake now not so blasé as her fingers—complete with purple nails—tapped the tabletop.

Mark cleared his throat. "Where'd you go last night? I came back in and you were gone. I was just gone a minute to tell Thad bye. I thought we were going to talk about computer graphics and the web design program at the college?"

She didn't take her eyes off the two adults. Adults? They were acting like two kids in high school. One of them pissed, the other not having a clue, but pissed now as well. All because of her. Well, to hell with that. Dad needed to get a freaking clue. Yes, she'd almost died, yes she was complicated and had...issues, but that didn't mean he could treat her like a twelve-year-old. Maybe she'd move out.

"Um, I had to go. I saw Lake and needed to tell her something and then figured I'd just go on home. Sorry. We'll have to get together another time."

He laid his hand on her shoulder and turned her around to him. "Fine, then tell me what the hell scared the crap out of you last night. I've never seen you like that before, Lys."

Last night...

The fog, the red, the feeling of pure unadulterated evil...

She shivered and shook her head. "N-nothing."

"Bullshit."

"Nothing." She couldn't talk about this. "Really. I need to go."

His hand on her arm was warm, but he didn't let her go. "You really need to tell me, I don't like thinking something is scaring you that badly." He waited until she met his gaze. "Or someone. Who scared you, Alyssa? And if you don't tell me," he said, pointing to the window, "I'm going to mention it to him. He loves you and wants to know you're safe and okay."

Okay? What the hell did that mean? She jerked her arm

away. "Just what is it with men?"

She whirled and saw that Lake had likewise jerked her hand from under Max's and stood talking, just as pissed off as her dad had been earlier.

Alyssa had no idea what they were saying, but she knew whom they were speaking of. Lake gave him one parting shot and then slammed into the coffee shop, making her way to the back. She paused, her heels no longer beating a staccato on the floor.

"Lake?" Alyssa asked, wondering if the woman would still talk to her.

"You want to meet with me?"

"Lake," her father warned from just behind them.

"Yes," Alyssa answered without glancing at him.

"Meet me upstairs in ten minutes. I need to cool off." Lake turned and pointed a finger at Alyssa's father. "You should have more faith in her and want her to get as much help as she can. She's going to need it."

Lake slid between Alyssa and Mark and slammed out the back door located beside the stairs that led up to her apartment.

"Way to go, Dad," Alyssa muttered. Then she poked her own finger at Mark. "And don't give me ultimatums. I don't like them. You want to tell him you saw me freak out on the sidewalk. Be my guest. I don't care."

She followed Lake's lead and slammed the back door to sit on the bottom steps that led to the apartment upstairs. The small back courtyard was quiet this morning and empty, thank God. Ten minutes until she could ask Lake how she knew all this stuff.

She glanced into the shop to see her father and Mark

talking to each other.

Idiots.

What was with men anyway? Maybe that would be the first question she'd ask Lake. Men could be such jerks! Her dad, Thad! Even Mark. Did they really just think women were there for their convenience, to listen to them give orders? Puh-leeze.

Max raked a hand through his hair. "What the hell did my daughter just mean by that?"

Mark looked at the door as if trying to decide the best route of escape.

Fat chance.

"Um. Well."

"Answer me. You and my daughter are friends but she's been through enough this last year. I won't allow anyone to hurt her."

At that, the young man leveled those clear blue eyes on him. "I won't either."

They glared at each other for a minute until Max again raked a hand through his hair, felt the muscle tick in his cheek.

"Women can be such a pain in the ass." He took three steps towards the front door, then turned back. "Can I get a coffee to freaking go?"

Mark bit his lip as if trying not to smile. "Yep. How about a large cup of African roast sure to zing you straight into a caffeine high?"

"Fine, but tell me, what did she mean?" Max, a bit calmer, leaned on the counter.

The kid—and he was a kid as far as Max was concerned—took a deep breath. "She was supposed to come over here last night. I saw her leave the house, watched her walk across the street then she turned and went down south. I waited a bit and then wondered where she went. But she didn't show and I started to get worried so I begged Nina to wait another ten minutes before ending her shift and went to look for Alyssa. She must have walked back up past the shop at some point. I finally saw her huffing and panting outside the coffee shop after she'd run from the opposite direction." Mark paused and frowned. "Something scared her, scared her bad." His bright blue eyes locked onto Max's. "Really bad, Max. I've never seen her that shook up. I brought her in here and sat her down, gave her some coffee." He rubbed his chin. "Then my brother showed up."

"Thad? Or Kevin?" Max asked.

"Thad. Kevin's still working up at the resort."

"I don't like Thad. He likes the girls too much and Alyssa doesn't need her heart broken."

Mark laughed. "Oh, he might break her heart if she let him, but she won't. She told him the same thing, to an extent. Anyway, I went out back to tell him bye, came back in and she was gone." Mark shrugged again. "That's it. That's all I know."

For a minute they stared at each other, then Mark turned and waited on the next customer.

Max blew out a breath. What the hell.

Women. And now Alyssa was pissed off at him. Well, what else was new? It wasn't his fault he cared and it offended her. He and Alyssa seemed to spend more time arguing—or her getting pissed at him and him trying to figure out what had her upset this time—than getting along.

But then the last time he'd been a permanent part of her life, she'd been nine and Timothy had been five. Pain, dulled and mixed with regret, would haunt him for the rest of his days.

He took another sip of coffee and shook off the thoughts. So she'd been scared last night. He'd thought that when she'd come in. But with Alyssa, he knew it could be any number of things to put that look of slick fear in her eyes—memories, nightmares, images she couldn't readily explain.

But what if this time it wasn't? What if this time it was real? As real as a semi running a red light and slamming into the side of his ex-wife's coupe and only one of them barely surviving?

Some evil, he knew, could never be seen. That didn't make the evil any less real.

Other evils were flesh and blood and just as deadly.

Now that his anger at Lake was passing, he knew it had been stupid on his part. Probably monumentally stupid. He rubbed a hand over his face. Maybe he was more worried about Alyssa than even he realized.

"You think someone hurt her?" Max finally asked, as he sipped his coffee, frowning. "Or tried to?"

"I don't know. I don't think so, but something sure as hell spooked her. Terrified her, actually."

Max just looked at him. "I'll ask her about it."

"No offense, but I don't think she's gonna tell you anything," Mark predicted.

"Probably not," Max agreed, "but I have to at least try."

Because he'd learned the hard way that not trying at least one more time was unacceptable.

Chapter Six

Lake paced her apartment. How dare he! The man was insufferable, and to think she'd actually been up half the night with him in her thoughts.

Ass.

Jerk.

Her phone rang.

"What?" she snapped.

"And a good and bright morning it is, too," Cora said, her voice trying for light and missing the mark.

"I've got dibs on pissy-bitch today, thank you very much. Pick another mood."

For a minute her friend said nothing and then sighed. "Okay, spill and then I get to share."

"He's a jerk. A machismo jerk. A know-it-all who doesn't know anything about...about...anything," she muttered and plopped down on the sofa, crossing her legs. She swung a foot out and in. A habit she'd had since childhood. She couldn't freaking sit still especially when she was aggravated or pissed off.

"Do I need to send Rogan down there to kick someone's ass? He would, you know. He will forever love you."

It made her smile. Rogan Duran and Cora were perfect for

each other and so in love it actually made her jealous. "No," she said, picking at the stitching on the arm of the microsuede sofa. "No, any ass needs kicking, I'll gladly do it myself."

"Okay, if you're sure. We're only a phone call away, you know. Oh, hang on..."

Lake heard muffled voices in the background.

"Sorry, as I was saying, if you change your mind, we ass-kick to please."

This time she chuckled. "Man I miss you guys. I needed this call. Maybe I should just come home."

"We miss you too," Cora said, her voice soft and convinced. "So, what did he do?"

She took a deep breath and tried to let it out slowly, but it didn't help. She was pissed. Very pissed. "The idiot questioned my conviction in what I do, first of all. He did that last night."

"Before or after you had him in bed."

"And then—" She blinked. "God, Cora, there wasn't a damn bed."

"With you, there never had to be."

"Bitch."

"Back at ya, babe."

Lake grinned. "Sooooo, as I was saying, he questioned my conviction while we were having dinner. A nice dinner too that he ruined. But we talked about it, ya know?"

"Talked about what?"

"If I really believe in what I 'sell', for the lack of anything else to call it."

A silent beat thrummed over the phone. "I'll leave that one alone, it's too easy and you're not in the mood." Another humming moment, then, "Okay, so he questioned you, basically what you believe, which by the way, is simply *who* you are.

Then what?"

"Then I said that it wasn't just a damned mask that I put on when it suited me. It was part of me, reading auras and believing in fate and psychics." She stood, waving a hand in aggravation. "Or whatever. The point is he questioned, I answered, thought we had it settled, and then he kissed me."

"The good part."

For a moment she thought back to the explosive kiss that she had wanted more of. "Yeah, it was good, great in fact, and the man is no doubt superb in bed, but that's all beside the point."

"Dear me. Lake just said that superb sex is beside the point." Cora's clear laughter rang over the phone as she clearly told whoever was there with her what Lake had just said.

Cora's chuckles still danced through the phone.

"This is so not funny, dammit. I need some—"

More giggles. "Yes, I've noticed. You're wound so tight..." More laughter.

Frustrated, Lake sighed and said, "When you get done laughing and want to know why I'm so pissed I could smother him with his own drop cloths, call me back."

She clicked the phone off. Damn it. Where was a—

The phone rang again.

"I'm sorry. Really," Cora said, not laughing, but Lake could still hear the smile in her voice. "I promise I will remain silent until you ask my opinion. Rogan left so I won't get in trouble for yelling our conversation at him. He misses you and your stories."

Yeah, right. "So anyway," Lake picked up as if never having left off, "here I was, and here he was, and he had a valid reason to worry. About my convictions, ya know?" She took another deep breath. "He's got a daughter, probably nineteen-twentyish, I can't remember, college age anyway." She closed her eyes and sat back down on the couch. "The girl is the most gifted I've ever been around, Cora. I mean I can not only see her aura, but *feel* it. Really feel it. And she doesn't have a clue, at least not that I've noticed. Well, to some extent." She stood again and paced to the window. "So I had mentioned to her that I'd like to talk to her and he's concerned that I'm merely playing her or scamming her or something, ya know? But I thought we cleared all that up."

"Last night, right?" Cora asked.

"Yeah, we discussed it over dinner then he kissed me and then I left."

"Wait. I have to ask."

"What?"

"This guy you've been eyeing for months finally took you out and then he kissed you but that's it? And it was a great kiss?"

Lake smiled, remembering it, then scowled. "On my old scale, at least a eight, if not a nine."

"No tens?"

"Ten was years ago, no one's ever met that one."

"Another story."

"Another time," Lake finished on a smile.

"Yet after you sleep with him, I feel confident he might move up."

"Possibly. If we ever get that far." Which she doubted. "Anyway, so we had plans to meet, right?" She went through the rest of it and stopped after she had told Cora about the feeling of darkness and evil that had reached out to the girl.

"What do you think it is?" Cora asked.

"I don't know. I really don't. Someone who isn't well-meaning, that's for damn sure. So after that I asked her if she wanted to join us and she agreed. Now this morning he's pissed because he said no one used his daughter to get to him and he resented that I had."

"Oh my. Is he still alive?" Cora asked.

"I'm not joking, Cora. I really liked this guy and he just...he's just..."

"A jerk."

For a minute neither said a word as Lake looked out her window to the courtyard below and the Taos Mountain beyond.

"But," Cora started.

"There are no buts."

"Not really, and it doesn't excuse his behavior, no, but maybe someone tried to chummy up to the girl before to 'get' to him. Face it, we're not exactly normal to believe in dreams, visions, auras. Maybe both he and his daughter were hurt before because of someone else faking belief in what simply comes natural to us."

She really hated voices of reason. "I was riding a great wave of mad."

"And so you should. He should not have jumped to conclusions. And it's not like the girl is ten or twelve or fifteen."

"No, but she is vulnerable. Not sure of herself, not really." And on that, she realized Alyssa was probably waiting on her, but she hated to get off the phone with Cora when Cora had phoned and said she needed to share something.

"What's up?"

A long silent moment passed. "Be careful, Lake. Just be careful, please."

"Oh, I will." She thought about the evil she'd felt. "I'm

different here, Cora. Lately I've felt off, or back on, whatever, and it's different. Before, there was a focused, yet fogged, way of seeing people, if that makes sense. But it's like after Simon and you and everything, I just shoved it all away. I couldn't trust myself."

"Lake—"

"I couldn't," she interrupted. "But now, here, I feel like I've *finally* found myself. Everything is different, sharper. The glaze is gone, or whatever. I still see auras, yes, when I try, but now I can feel them."

"Them?" Cora asked.

"Them. I can focus and read anyone if I want. But some are just *there*."

Cora cleared her throat. "Like?"

"Well, like Alyssa's. And whoever the darkness was. I didn't see his aura, but I felt it. He's dark, Cora." She shuddered. "Maybe even worse than Simon."

"Wonderful, that'll help me sleep at night." A breath huffed out. "I don't know if anyone is worse than Simon and we'll hope that you're wrong. I hope you're wrong." For a minute Cora didn't say anything, but Lake waited her friend out. "Lately, I've had dreams again, Lake."

Cora's gift was dreaming. And her dreams were not to be taken lightly.

"What about? Me?" she asked.

"I don't..." Cora sighed. "Just be careful, watch your back and forget Max. Either he's worth it, and you, or he's not. You can't 'make' him be worth it."

She smiled. "I know. Thanks, sweetie. I've got to go."

Alyssa checked her watch. She'd been daydreaming or

something because more time had passed than she'd realized.

A door opened at the top of the stairs and Lake stepped out holding a cell phone that she clipped to the side of her skirt in a cute little purple case with copper designs on it.

"Cool phone case."

Lake frowned. "What? Oh, yeah, thanks, a friend of mine made it."

"Knew you liked purple did they?"

Lake smiled. "Sorry, got a call from a friend and needed to vent."

Alyssa knew. "About Dad."

Those green eyes all but flashed fire. "Yes, about your father, idiot man. Well, don't just stand there, come on up."

Lake stepped back inside and left the door open. Alyssa hurried up the stairs and into the apartment. She'd been up here before. She'd helped Mrs. Howard clean it after other renters or weekenders had left, but it had been awhile.

She closed her eyes and took a deep breath. A peace shimmered around the apartment, slightly rippled—due, probably, to Lake's ire.

"Feel okay?"

Not feeling, but feel.

"Your anger has disturbed the peace," Alyssa said, just watching to see what the other woman would say to that.

Lake threw her head back and laughed. "Damned right it did, usually does." Then she focused those green, green eyes on her. "Do you always read a house? A room?"

Alyssa thought about it. "I guess. I used to but..."

"But?"

Sighing, she sat on the couch and picked on the leg of her

jeans. "You're real, right?" Then she saw it, felt Lake's aura almost burn, the edges going more orange, almost red around the purple and blues. "Sorry, I don't mean to be disrespectful, it's just that some people around here just do it for the money, a fun show so to speak." She shrugged. "Some locals are real. The Brothers Grimm. They're real, I think."

"What?" Lake filled some glasses with water, then sliced a lemon and dropped one in each glass. "There are really brothers named Grimm?"

Alyssa grinned. "No, that's just what I dubbed them. They have a shop a few blocks down and over, back in the alley. Very dark, leans towards the occult but cool. Lots of materials and stuff, books and research about auras, new age stuff, psychics, whatever."

"Are they truly knowledgeable or just there to sell to the public?"

She frowned. "I don't know, the shop seems real, has an energy. Sometimes good, sometimes not." She thought about it. "Yeah, I think they, or one of them, is more into the dark side of things, though maybe I'm wrong."

Lake's brows rose. "Really? Hmmmm…"

"Anyway, they believe me. The younger brother, Jay, he saw me walk into the shop several months ago and then just had some books for me sitting on the counter when I was ready to check out." She shrugged again, remembering. "He just knew."

"And you're wondering which category I fall into?"

Alyssa studied her for a moment more. "No, I guess I know, or I wouldn't be here, would I?"

She took the glass of water Lake handed her and sipped.

"Your father doesn't want you here. I don't think he believes in what I do."

"That's not it. There was this fortune teller..."

Lake laughed, the sound husky and real. Alyssa bet the men and boys alike really dug that laugh.

"That's what they all say."

"No, really there was." She twisted the cuffs of her knit jacket. Why was she nervous? Shaking off the anxiety, she said, "The fortune teller was nice. Really nice, actually. Her name was Shannon. She was sweet, brought us dinner and stuff. I'd just moved here and moved in with Dad and things were messed up. He'd been around when I was little. Then, after the divorce, he left and now here I was needing all this help and care and... Well, anyway, Shannon helped out a bit. She was nice, but she wanted to talk, to connect, and I just didn't want to." She scrunched her nose. "I think they'd been seeing each other before." She waved a hand. "It wasn't lasting, probably due to me. I couldn't have made things easy. Dad was in a bad place, not just with me but because the accident also killed my little brother. But Shannon tried, I have to give her that, and she was friendly enough, but it seemed fake."

"And your father figured it out and he wasn't going to put up with it."

She thought back to that time. "I guess. I was hyped on pain meds still and confused and..."

"Angry."

Angry didn't begin to cover the plethora of emotions that had raged through her. "Yeah, angry."

"You get counseling?"

Alyssa chuckled and then laughed, laughed until tears came to her eyes and her sides hurt. "I'm sorry, I'm sorry."

Lake took a slow sip of her water. "Don't apologize to me, dear."

"I've seen more shrinks than anyone else I know."

"Ahhh."

She stopped and Lake had a knowing smile. "Let me guess. Parents didn't understand, teachers definitely didn't, so thus something must be wrong when you could 'read' people. Or just knew things."

"I saw kids and people that no one else ever saw."

"That'll get them every time." The words were so deadpan that it took a minute to realize she'd been sarcastic.

"You see them?"

Lake shook her head. "No, I can only read people. Not like if they're lying or feel their pain or whatever, but I can sense some emotions if strong enough, and they have to be really strong. Auras for the most part are my thing. Just auras."

"You any good at it?"

"God, the honesty of youth." Lake studied her glass. "I used to be." She pulled the amethyst pendant back and forth on the chain and whispered, "I used to be."

Alyssa thought about that and tilted her head. "So to answer your question, yes, I've seen many, many shrinks. Who prescribed any drug you could dream up." She rubbed her arms. "At one point I couldn't stand it and thought I'd just end it."

"That would have been a damn shame, Alyssa." Lake's eyes narrowed and there was no pity, but anger there. "A stupid, selfish mistake."

"Yeah, I know that now, but God, I was so tired of no one listening, of no one believing."

"Your dad didn't?"

Alyssa shrugged. "He wasn't around. Only Mom and, no she didn't."

"I understand."

"Do you really?"

She smiled. "My parents haven't heard from me for years, because that is the way they want it. I'm strange and weird and don't fit into the family."

"Huh. Dad was never so...rigid about things like that. I think that was what finally pulled him and Mom apart. He didn't think I needed doctors. His grandmother was gifted, he said, maybe I got it from her. My mom wanted me to be more normal like my...my little brother, Timothy. He died in the accident with Mom."

Lake just listened as she suddenly talked, talked like she rarely did except with Dr. Wellbourne. "I'm seeing someone now. A parapsychologist."

"Is it helping?"

"Yeah, he kind of creeps me out sometimes, but yeah, he's made me see there's nothing really wrong with me. I'm just different. My brain is wired differently than other people to pick up things others miss."

Lake smiled. "Intuitive man."

"Yeah. So I guess I know you're real, but it's hard sometimes to believe." Why was that? "I mean, I know I *know* and yet I doubt. Why?"

"Oh, I'm well acquainted with that confusion."

"You?" No way. The woman was way too confident to ever doubt anything, let alone herself.

"Yep. Me."

"How? Why?" Alyssa knew she sounded disbelieving but she couldn't help it. The doubts drove her nuts. More than the things she saw, or knew, or sensed. The doubt was like a monster that sucked her energy.

Lake gave a half smile, not a happy one, and it didn't reach her eyes.

Alyssa sighed back into the plush sofa and closed her eyes. "Sometimes," she admitted. "I can't sleep."

"Nightmares." Lake didn't question, simply stated.

"Yeah."

"With our gift come curses."

"What's yours? Why don't you believe?"

"We are a pair," Lake muttered before standing and walking to look out the window. "I almost got a friend hurt."

"How?"

"Well, more like killed."

Alyssa frowned. "Wow."

Lake took a deep breath, the lines around her mouth tight.

Chills danced over Alyssa's skin and she could see them now, scars in Lake's aura that the memories must be bringing back.

"You don't have to tell me."

Lake didn't say anything. "I enjoy men. Not like I used to, and I don't mind being by myself, and I'm not saying it's okay to just go out and sleep with anyone," she added the last and turned to level an adult look at her.

Alyssa rolled her eyes. "I know that. God, you and Dad. You'd think I'd never heard of the *S* word before. I took the sex-ed classes, thank you."

Lake's grin was more real this time, but her aura was dimmed, dimmed greatly from what it had been before. "Yes, well, Simon seemed so...perfect."

The scars got deeper, darker. "He hurt you. Really hurt you."

"Not me, no, not really, but he was a very bad man and I *never* saw it. Never saw it in him. All that darkness." The last was whispered.

Alyssa shrugged. "Maybe you weren't supposed to."

"I guess not."

"He had a black aura." She'd read of them, though she'd never actually tried to find one.

"But I've seen black auras."

"I know, but I read this thing, this research some guy did about serial killers and how many of them have black auras, or parts of their auras are black. But the worst were the sociopaths. They didn't care, there was no feeling, no real—no real..." She trailed off, looking for the right word. "Not enough feelings and emotions to create a *true* aura. They were so dark, so soulless no one could really read them, or see them, or even sense them. Just that there was darkness. Maybe this person was like that."

"Oh he was. Never saw him, I felt him though." Lake rubbed her arms. "Just not at the most important moments. Like when I was with him."

"Really?" Besides the seriousness of the topic, she found herself very curious.

"Yeah, I felt the darkness, but it was just bits and pieces. Like...scattered confetti or something. I thought, 'Oh here's a bad boy I'd like to tangle with.' Then I started to notice he was deeper than I thought. Just glimpses that wouldn't tempt me but...chilled me." She shook her head. "Almost not in time. He took a friend of mine and almost killed her. So, yeah, I'm a little scarred and scared. He was a very bad man."

Alyssa thought about that. "What if you couldn't feel him, per se, but the effects he had on your friend?"

Lake sighed. "No, I sensed the danger before he took her."

"Maybe because he was already studying her?"

"What?" Lake asked, walking over to sit back down.

"Okay, I get the self-doubts you'd have, and maybe you're right and should have known and seen all. Fine." Alyssa shifted on the couch, not sure if she should say what she was feeling, but...to hell with it. Sighing, she continued, "But well, maybe it was like his energy was feeding off hers, off yours, and what you sensed was the marks he was leaving in her aura, the scars, like he left in yours."

For a moment, Lake just stared at Alyssa until she squirmed. Maybe she should just keep thoughts to herself.

Lake's gaze narrowed as she tilted her head and studied her. A slight frown pulled between her russet brows. "Go on. Please."

Alyssa started to think about what to say.

"Don't do that," Lake said.

"Do what?"

"Think too much. Just say whatever you're feeling, like you just did."

Alyssa was working on that in all areas of her life, but she'd weighed her words for so long, it was hard. "Okay. It's like that study said, right? About the evil being so black, so dark, no one could really, really see them or read them but they could feel a darkness. I thought of it like a black hole."

"Like astronomy?"

Alyssa sighed, relaxed. "Yeah. I mean, no one can see them. Not really. But they know they exist because of the effects of those things around them. The pull of a force. Ya know? Though unseen, the effects of the unseen are obvious."

Lake thought about it for a minute. "I never thought about it that way."

"Why?"

Lake frowned and the woman still managed to look sexy. "I have no idea. I just kept thinking that I should have seen, should have known."

"Yeah, because it always just works that way and we're omnipotent."

Lake laughed. "How old are you again?"

She grinned. "I'll be twenty next week, though I think Dad's forgotten."

"I doubt that. You are top where that man is concerned."

Alyssa thought about those words. "Maybe."

"Maybe? What does that mean? That man loves you and most importantly, *accepts* you. Thinks you like to shock people, but he loves you." Lake's eyes didn't waver from her. "That is a very precious thing. To have parents accept and love you no matter what."

"Can't argue that one." She'd been with her mother for years. Though she'd always love the woman, even with all her moods and issues, her mother had never really accepted her. Mom had always tried to shove her into a box she believed was appropriate.

"You already know that, though."

Alyssa just nodded.

"So why are you so mad?"

Alyssa smiled. "I'm a teenager, we're supposed to be moody and pissed at the world."

Lake chuckled. "Yeah, whatever. You're too old to be a moody teen. Maybe a moody kid dealing with trauma and the effects of its scars, but not because you're a typical moody nineteen-year-old. Nineteen-year-olds are past the moodiness generally and passionate about changing the world and politics." She shook her head. "Youth is exhausting."

"I don't really care about politics."

Lake's energies rippled again across the air and through the normally peaceful home.

"So you'll talk to me? Teach me stuff?"

Lake just looked at her. "I think the teaching may be two way. And honestly, I think you just need more confidence."

"That's what my shrink says."

For a minute, they both enjoyed the silence. She wanted to ask Lake about the other night, but didn't know how. To hell with it.

"You felt him too, didn't you?" Alyssa asked.

Lake held her stare. "Yes."

"He's evil. He's powerful. He'll hurt me, if he can." Why she felt that, she wasn't sure, but she did. She knew it.

Lake's mouth tilted ruefully, her expression more in agreement than in contradiction. "Not if we don't let him."

"No, not if we don't let him." Alyssa sighed. The words sounded good, but she knew sometimes there was no stopping fate. That inner knowledge warned her that he—whoever he was—would hurt her.

Chapter Seven

He waited and watched. He wanted her. The need to have her soon was consuming him. But he'd have to wait. It wasn't the right time and if anything still worked inside of him, it was his gut, that whisper of instinct that still called to him, that inner voice hissing that this was not the time to take her. Waiting would be better.

He nodded as he thought of her. Her image floated into his thoughts. Her soft skin, that scent that was both woman, yet still with a hint of child mixed in. Heady stuff that.

She knew. She actually knew he was present. There had been one other who had known he was watching, waiting, moving in... He'd taken him from Colorado after he'd tracked the boy down through the internet. The transfer had released the young man's power after he'd taken him to dinner. That one had been fun all around, different, as it had been a boy instead of a girl, but the charge had been there.

Pain bit deep inside his skull. He rubbed his temple, but it did no good. Time marched through him, through his being, like a giant clock.

Tick.

Tick.

Tick.

He had to have her soon, but not too soon. He wanted to stretch it out, enjoy it, have fun with it. And he would. No one would know. No one would suspect, and those who did, the girl and the woman—pretty, that one—would hardly be listened to.

There was power in disbelief and that power aided his cause.

He smiled. There was a bright side to having issues like his. Abilities like theirs were real, but few believed, and even those who claimed to believe rarely put stock into it.

To play and bring the power onto a higher level? Emotions fed power and the rush...

Desire thrummed through his body and he wanted, needed a release. But damn it all if he could actually have one. The meds took too much from him.

He wanted his life back.

He would have his life back. No matter how many he had to take. No matter how long he had to hunt. If he had to move at some point, fine. He'd moved before. Granted, never for this reason. But desperate times called for desperate measures didn't they?

He took another deep breath and thought of her. Her short dark hair all mussed, those gray eyes flashing fire, anger and hope.

Hope.

That emotion alone was almost hotter at times than all others. In the end, as her essence became his, which emotion of hers would cover her? Or would she be a mixture of many?

Either way, he knew without a doubt her transfer would be the greatest of all.

The rush ran through him just at the mere thought.

Soon...

Chapter Eight

Max paced back and forth, his mind not even remotely on anything dealing with the gallery. He had an appointment in— he checked his watch—shit. Now.

He walked from the back office into the main area of the gallery. Where was the one o'clock?

Lake.

Had he handled that situation wrong?

No.

He had a damned right to protect his daughter.

Yes. Okay, maybe there had been a better way to handle that situation.

His issues? She'd accused him of painting her with his own issues. What the hell had that meant? Okay, maybe he had done just that.

Lake wasn't Shannon. Shannon had meant well, and God knew the woman had tried but even before Alyssa had moved here, he'd known he and Shannon weren't a long-time item. There simply was no way he could picture it, and he'd never been able to put his finger on just why.

But even after Shannon, there had been others who he'd simply known were trying to get to him through his daughter. The first shrink Alyssa had gone to here. When Alyssa knew the doctor wasn't going to work for her, the therapist made her move on him. The woman was also a sex therapist. He shuddered. Then there was the lady who'd worked in the Wiccan shop last summer—what had her name been? Something that started with an *N*. Hell if he could remember. After two dates she'd told him how she could really help his daughter.

Lately, his dating track sucked.

He scrubbed his hands over his face and looked across the street. There out on the deck above the coffee shop stood his daughter and Lake. What had they done all day? Since he hadn't heard from either of them, let alone had he seen his daughter, they'd apparently spent the morning together. Probably had lunch too. Girl talk and God only knew what else. Whatever they had done or were doing, they appeared to enjoy each other's company. Currently, they were talking, then Alyssa threw her head back and laughed.

He frowned. How long had it been since he'd seen her do that?

He had no idea. Had she ever done that with him? No, not to his knowledge. And he seriously doubted she'd ever been able to do that with her mother. But she was laughing with Lake, and if she was laughing with Lake, that meant she was at ease with her.

There was food for thought.

Hell.

Maybe both of them were right and it had nothing to do with him.

For now, he'd just watch them. His daughter had been through too much, had too much heartache already to be put through anymore. No matter who it was from, he wouldn't stand for it.

But if she could connect with someone...

The bell over the door clanged as a kid no older than his daughter walked through the door.

Max sighed. Not another art student? Kid probably was. He really hated to disappoint the kids. They had this idea that if they couldn't make it in Taos, they'd have a piss-poor chance at making it elsewhere, which was stupid. Art was subjective.

Taos had its own style. Customers both local and visiting had an idea of what they'd find in a Taos gallery, and he was also a businessman. So even if the art spoke to him, unless he knew he could sell it, chances were he'd turn them down and try to explain it all to them. Sometimes he was successful, and sometimes he wasn't.

Please don't let this one be a crier.

"Mr. Gray?"

"Please bring your stuff over here."

The kid shoved a pair of wire-rimmed glasses up his nose and placed his large attaché case on the side desk below the lights in front of the windows.

Max hated and loved this part. Would this be something he'd want?

Or something he'd hate?

The anticipation was almost like...

He glanced through the window across the street. Lake now stood alone on the second floor and she was staring across the street at him.

He lifted his hand though he knew, from the shadows cast by the portico that lined this set of shops, that she'd never see him.

Apologize whispered through his mind.

Yeah, he'd have to do that. Groveling would probably be

involved. He hated groveling.

"So what do you think?"

Max took a deep breath and looked down.

Not what he was expecting. He gave the black and white photos more attention.

They were not the normal door or windows, mountains or wildlife the locals normally went for. Clean lines and bareness that was known as the Santa Fe style. Nor was this guy trying to imitate O'Keefe. Thank God. Max had lost count of O'Keefe wannabes.

These were still shots of people. Here in Taos. The local flavor was still there. With the lighting and location there was still that feeling of bareness and clean lines, but it was subtle. The people were drinking coffee, talking on patios. Walking and holding hands at night, in the evening. He picked up the next one, which had a group of friends laughing at a street corner and waiting to cross while the man in the background was selling *ristras*.

The flavor of Taos was in local landmarks clearly seen in the photos. The people, though, made the photos come alive, and the lighting, the shadows gave the photos...something. An essence. A life. He grinned and flipped to the next one. He glanced at the kid, who had paled. Max held his tongue.

"No *Sangre de Cristos*?" he asked, wondering where the one mountain shot had to be.

The kid shrugged. "I figured you see enough of those. I have a few, but it's always in the background."

"People-watching, huh?" He flipped to another of lovers under an arch, lit by the street light behind them.

He was rarely impressed. He gave the kid more of his attention. "I'm sorry, what was your name again?"

"Jonathan Murbanks."

"Murbanks." He nodded. "I think we'll just say these are Murbanks. A sign in black and white. Or black and gray, to keep with the theme of your photos."

"Wow. Really? Really?" The young man's face lit with relief, excitement and laughter. And when he laughed, Max realized he wasn't so young after all. Strange.

"How old are you?"

"Twenty-six."

Not so much a kid, no, but still young with life.

"You look nineteen, or twenty."

"Good genes." Dimples pitted his cheeks when he smiled.

"Something."

They looked through the photos again and he picked the ones he really wanted to showcase first, let Jonathan choose a few more and then made another appointment for him to bring by other prints. "When you bring the next batch, we'll decide which ones to enlarge."

That tingle ran through his system that he'd found something, was onto something. He'd found another one.

Max smiled and felt good for the first time all morning.

"Thank you, Mr. Gray."

"Who else turned you down?" he couldn't help asking.

Jonathan's mouth screwed to the side. "Well, I figured this was where I wanted to showcase, so I'd come here first and then see what happened."

"Confidence." He motioned to the photos. "It shows."

"Hey I need—" Alyssa strode out from the back office and stopped. She stood staring at Murbanks for a full ten seconds. Max looked at the artist he was going to sign to see what the guy thought and—oh hell.

Jonathan's eyes had widened and then he smiled. "Hello."

Alyssa shook her head. "Umm. Hello." Finally she blinked and focused back on him. "Sorry, for interrupting, I just needed to talk to you about something, but it can wait."

Her eyes hadn't stayed on him, but had instead slid over and froze on Murbanks.

Max took a deep breath and wondered what the hell he was supposed to do. He'd seen her off on a date with the lady's man—Thad. And thank God that had gone nowhere. He'd have alienated his daughter if he'd killed the kid.

Mark. Mark he liked, did like. Nice boy.

Mr. Murbanks should not have this affect on his daughter. And he'd just told the starving artist he'd carry him. Complicated crap bothered him.

Alyssa walked closer. Thankfully, she'd dressed normal today. Or as normal as she got. She only had one piercing in her brow. Her clothes were tasteful yet eclectic in their tie-dyed color patterns. Then again, this was Taos, what was normal really?

From the corner of his eyes, he watched as the new artist ran his gaze over Alyssa once, twice and then again.

"For the love of..." Max muttered.

Alyssa quickly flipped through the photos, her brow furrowing as she concentrated. She flicked a look to the young man and then to him with a question in her eyes.

"You like?" he asked his daughter.

She studied the photos yet again. "Actually, I do. At first, you just kind of think, huh, pictures. Then one grabs you. And you look closer." She continued to look through them, giving closer attention to each one. "They're local, which is cool, yet not stereotypical with the mountains or more pueblos. Yet you get the..." She turned to the next one of a couple kissing at night beneath an arch. "Flavor."

Murbanks cleared his throat and made his move, stepping closer. "That's what I was aiming for. I wanted people to get the feel of the southwest, but not have it pushed in their faces." He shoved his hands in his pockets.

As a man he should probably feel sorry for the kid, but as a father, he really couldn't drum up the sympathy.

"Plus," Murbanks continued, leaning a little bit closer to Alyssa, "I like to people-watch."

Normally, Alyssa didn't like to be too close to people. Max kept waiting for her to move or step away. Instead she only looked at Murbanks.

Max knew what was coming. He smiled to himself and crossed his arms over his chest.

"Your aura is interesting," she said softly.

Max frowned. That wasn't how she normally delivered the news. She went for shock. For the awe factor.

This was different.

Jonathan smiled. "I've heard that before." He studied her and took a deep breath. "So you like my photos?"

"Y-yeah. I uh, I do." She looked back down at the stack she held in her hands.

"Cool."

And this was where he set a few things straight. Max cleared his throat. "Mr. Murbanks. Meet my daughter, Alyssa."

For a minute there was nothing, then Murbanks blinked, blinked again and said, "Daughter?"

Alyssa's laughter danced out.

Murbanks's eyes shifted to meet Max's. "I'll get you those

photos tomorrow."

With that, Max watched as Alyssa helped the man pack up. She even walked him to the door. Normally, Max would have been pleased to see her taking charge like this, to agree and point out the artistic qualities of a client's work. But hearing her stroke the man's ego just sat wrong with him.

Then again, she was nineteen and he figured it was only going to get worse for him.

Daughters. Almost twenty-year-old daughters...

He had heartburn.

Alyssa strode into The Book Emporium & More.

She took a deep breath and savored the scent of old musty books, new books, incense and just a feeling of peace. She loved this place.

"If it isn't our beautiful Alyssa," Yancey said, his smile wide as his face.

Yancey wasn't as tall as she, more barrel-like than bodybuilder and perfectly happy in his roundness. He'd always reminded her of a bulldog. Maybe it was the jowls. With his strange golden eyes, she often wondered where his ancestors came from. His brother, a sweet if somewhat simple man, wasn't as round. In fact, the last time she'd seen Jay, he'd been pale and looked as if he was losing weight. The brothers did share the same strange eyes, though. And though Jay, she knew from dealing with him, was clearly not the smarter of the two, he was still a sweet man. He loved books as much as his brother. But he was weird.

To be honest, Alyssa didn't like coming into the store if only

Jay was working. It wasn't that she had a fear or aversion to those with special needs, but Jay had a way of watching her that unnerved her. However, she didn't want to be rude to the guy, so she was always nice, always polite and never stayed more than just a few minutes if he was the one running the shop. There was just something about those strange yellow eyes following her around the shop that tightened her stomach and made her breath catch.

Yancey claimed they were of Romany descent. She'd looked that up on the internet and realized he meant gypsies. But what? Eastern European? Central European? Italian? And what exactly were Romanies? Did they originate in Rome? These were questions she wanted to ask him, but she was never certain if they were appropriate or rude.

Her mother would have said rude.

Of course her mother wouldn't have let her even look at this shop, which was neither here nor there.

She'd probably have to bring up this little episode of thinking with her shrink. Regression, especially thoughts of her mother's approval was never a good thing. Never. Nope.

"Hey, Yancey. How's it going?" She glanced behind the counter to the empty stool. "Where's Jay?"

"He wasn't feeling so well today," Yancey muttered, shaking his head. "You know Jay. The air got cold and he's not feeling very well. He doesn't think the wind is blowing right. Or so he says." His rounded shoulders shrugged. "He'll be fine in a day or so."

A chill danced down her spine. "O-okay. Well, let him know I hope he gets to feeling better." She had the urge to get out of the shop, but she sometimes had that urge when she stepped in here. *Thanks, Mom.* No, she'd stay, to see if there was anything new.

She'd already bought several tarot decks. Two to practice on, to see which ones she liked better, which had a better feel to her. She wasn't of the belief that all decks were the same. They might all have the same pictures, but they were *not* all the same. She knew this without a doubt. How she knew it, she wasn't sure, but there she was anyway. She also had this beautiful gold inlay deck, which she'd found in the back corner with a layer of dust on it. When she'd asked Yancey if she could buy it and what the price was, he'd just smiled and told her to take them.

She never used those. Not really used them. She looked at them, admired them and loved to simply touch them, but she never really used them.

She'd also purchased an old birch wand. She didn't believe in witches or wizards, in wands or potions or whatever, maybe not even tarot, though tarot was interesting. No, the wand was just a cool stick with a wicked purple crystal on the end, which she would pry out one day and then ditch the stick more than likely.

"What's your dad been up to? I saw him and the Howards' newest renter going at it outside the coffee shop." Yancey stacked three books on the counter and put a bundle of herbs on it as well.

"Yeah, well, that's Dad for you. Throwing romance away." She grinned. "He's good actually. Finding new talent or trying to."

"No lack of wannabes in this town."

She smiled at Yancey and picked up a book on herbs. Herbology was another interest she had. There were almost as many holistic or organic food stores here in Taos as there were galleries. She didn't want to buy a weed for this or that ailment or need just because the bottle said it was good for her. She wanted to actually know and understand what these things were used for. Her shrink and her dad both wanted her to be interested in things, to have a hobby. For now, her hobbies varied and included learning and reading about various topics.

"That's a good one," Yancey told her.

She flipped through the book, noticed it not only gave directions to make tonics and infusions but also topical creams. There were both drawings and photos of the plants, with bold cautions and warnings. Huh. She skimmed on through it. "I'll take it."

While he rang her up, Yancey asked, "So what are your plans? Decide on the graphic arts school?"

She shook her head. "I've no idea yet. It'll come to me. For now, I'm just helping Dad and that's enough."

"Getting your bearings is important," Yancey told her. "It's always important to know where you stand and who you are."

So it was.

"Any new friends? I heard you and that Lake lady were spending time together."

Yancey always had the latest gossip. The fact people wanted to talk about her was both intriguing and disturbing.

"Yeah, she's really nice."

Yancey leaned closer. "I heard she's gifted too. Ran her own shop in Sedona. You might find that friendship useful," he added.

"Well, Lake's nice and she's helping me with some stuff." She wasn't really in the mood to chat. "Thanks, Yance. I've got to get going." She grabbed her bag and shoved out the door. The alley as usual was dark and dreary. She looked up and noticed the low-hanging snow clouds. She was so ready for spring. Real spring and melting, not more snow. But it was going to snow.

She knew it. When she reached the edge of the alley that led onto the street, she took a deep breath and the bands around her chest loosened.

Maybe she'd wait awhile before she went back into the bookstore again. She glanced over her shoulder. Why did she seem to feel more darkness when she visited it now? Why did a place that once called to her, seem to turn her off now?

Confidence...

Lake said to believe in herself. Time to try that. She *would* try doing that. So if the bookstore bothered her this much, she'd just not come again—for a while anyway.

Taking a deep breath, she walked back towards the gallery.

Max sighed and knocked on the door. He waited and then waited a bit more. Finally, the door jerked open and Lake stood on the other side, glaring at him.

He was used to seeing her in purple, or copper, though usually black. But today she wore an oversized cream sweater, the top bunched and thick around her neck, the bottom hanging past her hips. Those long, trim legs were encased in some sort of creamy tights or something. Leggings. His daughter called those leggings. Whatever. Her thick red braid lay over her shoulder. Her eyes seemed even greener this evening.

Eyes that still glared at him.

Hell.

"Can," he said, clearing his throat, "I come in?"

She tapped her long purple nails against the doorframe—

once, twice—then she stepped back and let him in. Thankfully. It was cold outside.

"Thanks."

She shut the door behind him, never taking her eyes off him. "If I hadn't let you in, you'd have wanted to stay and talk on the stoop and then I'd be colder than I am already and that's never a good thing."

"Yeah, it's cold." He jerked his head to the large picture window and balcony doors that overlooked the front street and his gallery. "The snowstorm is supposed to hit soon."

"That's what I heard." She stared at him for a minute more and then walked towards the fireplace and tossed in another log.

"You want a cup of tea or coffee? Water?"

Twilight was falling, the evening going soft pink-purple. He'd closed his shop early and had hurried over here thinking he needed to speak to her. What the hell had he been thinking?

"Whatever's fine. Or nothing." He shoved his hands in his pockets, rocked up on the balls of his feet and said, "Look, I wanted to apologize."

"Really?" She sat on the deep plush couch and sipped from a thick blue mug.

"Not gonna be easy," he muttered, looking at the floor.

"Honey, I'm *never* easy."

He glanced at her from beneath his lashes. "Oh, of that I'm very certain."

A smiled tugged at the corners of her mouth.

"I'm sorry, Lake. I didn't mean to be so rude and..." And what?

"A jerk?" she supplied.

"A jerk. An ass."

113

"A fool." She smiled, though it didn't reach her eyes, as she looked at him over the rim of her mug. "Though ass works too."

He took a deep breath and strode to the fireplace, stretching his hands out towards it. "And I just wanted to apologize and explain that you were right. I was painting you with my issues. I don't mean to, but..."

"But?" she asked.

He shrugged. "When Alyssa is mentioned, I just get...I get..." Hell. He raked his hands through his hair.

"Protective. Worried. Scared."

The woman was no idiot. Probably why he liked her. "Yeah, all those things."

"I know," she said softly. When he turned back to her, she continued, "I'm sorry too. I have a quick temper in some regards. Not most, but you question my integrity and I can be quick to jump in."

"I noticed."

For a moment neither said a word. Finally she patted the cushions beside her.

Thank God. He took a slow breath, walked over and sat down. "I didn't think I'd get past the 'I'm sorry' before you slammed the door shut on me."

She grinned and took another drink. "I thought about it."

He sat back and put his arm on the back of the couch. After only a moment's hesitation, she leaned into him, pulling her legs up under her. The fire crackled and danced as they simply watched it.

"Can we try again?" he asked quietly. Hoping. Maybe she didn't want to have anything to do with him anymore.

She sighed and rested her head on his shoulder. "I like Alyssa and we're going to meet at least once a day for however long she wants to."

He thought about that. He scratched the side of his mouth with his finger. "Okay." He might be worried about her, but he'd seen something that day he hadn't seen in a long time. Still staring at the flames dancing, he said, "I saw you, both of you out on the balcony. She laughed." The flames, dark blue, licked the log. "I haven't seen her laugh like that in so long, I honestly can't remember." A lump formed in his throat. "She used to be carefree when she was very little, and she'd laugh like that. I couldn't hear her, not from the gallery, but still, I knew what it would sound like."

She breathed deeply and patted his thigh. "She knows. I'm not trying to take anything from you. I'm not a threat to your daughter, you know, or your relationship with her."

He swallowed and turned his head to look at her. "You wouldn't mean to be. But I worry about what she'll do when you go back to wherever, Sedona, wasn't it? When you go back there to run your shop, what will she do?"

For a moment she didn't say anything, then she shifted so they more faced each other than not. "Max. I don't know what is going to happen tomorrow, let alone later than that. I've never lived that way. Alyssa's nineteen and if I go back to Sedona, then she can visit if she wants. There're also these inventions known to many as the phone and email and texting. I'm not going to drop her. You can't wall her up, Max. You'll put her in danger if you do that."

He frowned. "I know. I remember something my grandmother said once, and my mom agreed with her. That Alyssa needed to experience things with her talents, openly and freely without any threat or anxiety of rejection, for her to truly understand who she was."

"She's got a pretty damned good handle on who she is, who

others are."

He raised a brow.

"Really. Thanks to *you*."

"Oh, I don't know about that."

She lifted her hand and ran her fingers through the hair on the side of his head. "I do. She said as much, though I won't tell you anything else we talked about. But she loves you, and I think it says a lot that she's comfortable enough with you to discuss some of the things that happen to her, that she experiences."

He hadn't really thought of that. "Still, doesn't feel like enough."

She smiled. "Not to you, maybe."

He thought about that for a while.

He reached for her hand and kissed her wrist, watching as her eyes darkened. "So are we okay?"

"I don't know," she said, and looked into his eyes. "Are we?"

"It feels like it," he admitted.

She took a deep breath. "Max. I don't know how to tell you..." Her lips pressed together before she continued. "You've been honest with me, so I'll be honest with you. I like Alyssa. I see some of me—very little, granted—in her. But that vulnerability, wanting acceptance, is something I understand all too well. I have this urgency to help her, this feeling that she's going to need my help."

"For—"

She held up her hand and interrupted him. "I like you, I like her. I'm not using either one of you to get to the other, and I don't want to have to worry that I'm going to offend or upset you because of something I did with your daughter and—"

"As long as you're not getting her drunk or into drugs, or

setting her up for sex dates, I'm good."

She blinked. "I'm not that bad an influence." She tilted her head. "Well, maybe once upon a time, but not in a long, long time, thank you very much."

He took a deep breath. "Or into the dark arts."

This time, she blinked three times. "Dark arts?"

He sighed and sat up, put his elbows on his knees. "My grandmother and mother were gifted." To hell with it. Honesty. He wanted honesty, he'd have to give it as well. "Upon occasion I get feelings, or intuitional guides. I get all that. But I also know that some of this stuff can pull you in, way in and be very, very dangerous. I don't want Alyssa there."

"I'm not into the occult, though that probably depends on who you'd ask."

"No, I get it." He raked his hands through his hair again.

"I promise not to get her drunk, high, or strung out. Nor will I push her into any sexual situations, or into the dark occult."

He huffed a breath and stared at the red threads of the woven rug on the floor. "I'm being stupid, aren't I?"

She laughed. "No. Well, maybe just a little. She's on the cusp of adulthood and is going to experiment with things we adults would rather she didn't."

"Nineteen going on forty." He leaned back, feeling more relaxed than he had in a long time.

"She's an old soul."

He grinned. "My grandmother used to say the same thing." He opened his eyes and stared at her. Giving in to impulse, he reached up, tucking a strand of hair behind her ear before gently pulling her towards him.

"You know what else pissed me off today?" he asked

quietly.

She shook her head. "Besides my charming self?"

"I didn't get to do this, this morning." He closed the distance between them and kissed her. The fire crackled and popped.

She tasted like coffee and dark secrets. Secrets he wanted to learn, and understand. Secrets he wanted to discover and explore, very, *very* slowly.

"And I was worried I would never get to do this again." He kissed her, long and hard. "You taste good," he said against her mouth.

"So do you."

The kiss turned from merely tasting to something more. He wasn't sure which one of them started it, but soon all he could see, taste, feel, was Lake.

Her mouth slanted over his again and again as her tongue dueled and parried with his. Just as he started to pull back, she nipped his lip. "Nu-uh. You're not going anywhere. Not yet."

She wrapped her arms around him and climbed on top of him, pushing him back into the couch.

He looked at her, at the wicked gleam in those amazing green eyes.

"Promise?" he asked, leaning up to nuzzle the side of her neck. She smelled of some scent he couldn't pinpoint, heady and dark, and tempting as hell.

"And then some." She leaned her head back, but he tugged her closer and licked a line from her collarbone up to her ear, gently pulling the lobe between his teeth and nibbling.

His hands found the bottom of the large sweater and he slipped beneath. Finally. Her skin was warm and silky soft. He wanted to taste every last inch of her.

Her fingers played with the hair at the back of his neck, sending shivers down his spine from the simple contact.

"This is sad," he muttered.

"I was thinking the same thing."

He leaned back slowly, leaving his hands under her sweater, slowly caressing from her back to her ribcage and up to just shy of her breasts.

"Really? And why is that?"

A slow, sexy grin on those wide lips made him think of all the things he'd love to do with that mouth. "Oh, just that it's either been a really, really long time or you're gonna be great in bed."

He leaned in and nipped her chin, kissed down the side of her neck as his hands spanned her waist, squeezing her hip bones. Her moan pulled a smile from him. Desire thrummed through his system. He wanted to take, but he also wanted to spend hours enjoying her. "I want to know all your secrets." He trailed his fingers back and forth beneath her breasts, the lace of her bra light and caressing against his fingertips. "Exactly how long has it been for you?"

He cupped those glorious breasts and realized she overflowed his hands. He took a deep breath.

"Uhhh..."

"That long, huh?"

"Umm. No. Several months, but not..."

He slipped his fingers just beneath the edges of lace and traced back and forth across the globes of breasts he couldn't wait to see.

"So you think I'll be great in bed." He licked the rim of her ear and she shuddered.

"God, I hope so."

Her mouth found his, her fingers lost in his hair as she deepened the kiss.

"Personally," he whispered between kisses and nibbles, "I'm pretty damned sure we're going to kill each other once we get to that point."

She shifted so that she fit more snugly against him and, God, if he couldn't feel the heat of her through his jeans. He wanted her now.

"At least we'll die happy." She rocked against him and he growled as he kissed her deeper, his hands pushing her bra up so that he could feel...

"I want to see you," he said, shoving her sweater up.

She leaned back, letting him push the hem up. Just as he glimpsed the undersides of her glorious breasts someone knocked on the door.

Thump. Thump. Thump.

She jerked her sweater down.

He growled. "Tell whoever the hell it is to go away."

She raised a brow and wiggled again, rubbing against the biggest hard-on he could remember having in a long damn time.

"Should I?"

Thump. Thump. Thump. "Lake?"

Alyssa. Shit.

Lake scrambled off his lap and he realized he'd better just stay sitting down. Taking a deep breath, he smiled as she yelled, "Just a sec!" She pulled her bra back into place and gave him a lopsided grin. "Someone said something about suspense, right?"

"Suspense?" He stared at her. "Maybe I'm reevaluating that."

She laughed and walked to the door.

"We're good, right?" he asked her.

She grinned at him over her shoulder and all he wanted to do was kiss the woman senseless again.

What the hell was his daughter doing here?

Sighing, he closed his eyes and leaned his head back, listening as Alyssa's voice drifted through the room.

"Sorry, I had to see you to ask a question about—" She dropped off. Her boot heels clicked across the wooden floor. "Dad's here. And umm... Damn. Sorry. I'll just come back later and—"

"Nonsense." Lake's voice sounded amused. "Come on in. We were just trying to decide what we wanted for dinner. Any suggestions?"

"Nah. I'm not hungry and—"

"Rule number one is to stay healthy. If you're healthy, you can control your gift better and if you're not, it's more liable to control you. So you're eating with us. End of discussion. And since I can't cook, I'm wondering where we should go to eat."

He could fix dinner.

"Italian. Something Italian sounds really, really good," Alyssa walked into the living room and said, "Sorry, Dad."

"For what?" He patted the sofa beside him. Alyssa's face was red, something he rarely saw. He'd embarrassed his daughter? Life was good.

"Oh, nothing. So you're paying, right?"

"No," Lake said from behind her, "I am."

"No," Max said, standing up. "I am."

"And the fun begins," Alyssa muttered.

Fun.

"Oh!" Lake said, poking Alyssa in the shoulder. "This is

going to be a blast. You know what? We can practice."

Alyssa's brow rose, complete with an eyebrow stud that twinkled blue in the lights. "Practice?"

Lake's laughter floated through the air and caressed him like it shouldn't since his daughter was in the room, but damned if he wasn't turned on anyway. "Practice what exactly?"

Then Alyssa laughed. "You know, you're right. I've never had anyone I could share this all with. I can. We can."

"We can see which auras are brighter."

He shook his head, already worrying about dinner ahead. "Exactly what are you two talking about?"

They looked at each other and grinned. "Nothing." They both answered him in all-too-cheery voices.

"Uh-huh." He stood up, found his coat and pulled it on as Lake shrugged into her dark coat as well. "You two play nice."

"Nice is boring, Dad."

His eyes met Lake's and he had the same thought, then shook it off as he realized who said it.

"Nice is nice, thank you very much. And since you're my daughter, nice you will remain."

She only snorted and then said to Lake, "He's hopeless isn't he?"

"Pretty much, but I still have hope for him."

Chapter Nine

He leaned in closer to her, sniffing the light scent of her skin. Candy and coffee. Teenage girls always smelled the same to him, no matter what perfume they wore or shampoo they used, or what they decided to eat or drink. Innocence. It was the scent of innocence and he reveled in it, sweet as candy and just as alluring. Desire thrummed through him, hot and thick, but damned if he could do anything about it.

She whimpered behind the gag he'd been forced to use on her. A cute little scarf she'd had on, in a rainbow of colors. Now the rainbow bit into the sides of her face, her cheeks, her pale hair.

The late evening light didn't reach far here, deep in the canyon. He wasn't far from the resort, but this time of year, people came and went so often, no one paid attention.

Did he care if they found her?

Her eyes, wide and terrified, locked on him, like an oil painting that had hung in his childhood home. He hated eyes that followed, eyes that stared.

The bright blue eyes, which had laughed and questioned earlier, were no longer laughing. Eyes told stories. In hers, he wanted to smile at the fear, at the knowledge he could see in the depths. Questions. Knowledge. Fear. Pleading. So many emotions, and all he could read in her eyes.

"Shhh..." He lightly licked the edge of her jaw. "You're a special, special girl. Did you know that?"

Her eyes squeezed shut. He ran his hand over her chest, now bare of the sweater she'd been wearing earlier. He'd cut the blue garment off as soon as he'd gotten her in the back of the minivan. And it had been so easy. He *loved* spring break, hell any holiday weekend. There were so many to choose from at those times. The hunting was so *easy*. This girl had been here for a last ski vacation. Just a quick trip into town, taking the day off from skiing with her friends. Out all alone. Stupid, stupid.

"You should have stayed with your friends. Didn't anyone ever tell you there's safety in numbers?" He guessed not. "But then, you were sent to me," he whispered.

He'd known the moment he saw her. Her aura, bright and yellow, had shimmered, reminding him of summer, of things to come, of hope. Her laughter had danced in the air and he knew. Just knew.

The need in him arose until he'd had to listen, to appease. To gain more energy. This one he'd had to have now. Had to take now.

Her feet were bound, as were her hands. He'd laid the seats flat earlier in the day, and wasn't it handy that he had? A sign. A part of him had known, had known what was to come. His powers were coming back after all. He smiled at the thought and wished they would come back even quicker. He ran his hand over her trembling biceps. He loved his presents bound. There was just something...arousing and besides it was so much easier this way, he'd learned. So much easier to do with them as he would. Pose them so he could see.

But he was losing the light.

Pain sliced through his skull, hot as a searing knife. He bit down and took a deep breath.

She moaned again behind her gag and he again leaned down over her. "You're so pretty. I knew the moment I saw you, special one, that you were for me." He kissed her soft pale brow, felt her shudder. "You are special. Think of that. And know that what you have, I will always, always cherish."

He sat up, pulled her up into a half-sitting position, but still straddled her legs. It would hardly do for her to get some traction, would it? Not that it mattered, they were lying on plastic. Not that he planned to shed her blood, he wasn't a violent person after all. But still, he didn't want any messes.

He cupped her face, tilted it one way, then the other. "So pretty."

He jerked the gag down and kissed her, kissed her hard, as he gripped her neck and squeezed. Squeezed through the gasp that sucked air from his own lungs.

He loved this part. This *rush*.

The transfer...

She thrashed her head, but he was expecting that and kept his mouth tight over hers. Her body bucked and twisted. But half reclining, she was neither sitting up enough to fight him nor lying down enough to twist away.

Twist and fight she did. Her arms trembled. Her legs kicked, or would have if he hadn't been sitting on them. He tightened his hold on her, squeezed even harder, the soft muscles of her neck, the tendons, giving beneath his hands. Then her larynx snapped beneath the pressure.

She was a fighter.

Blood rushed through his veins, hot and fast, faster and faster, pounding against the inside of his skull. Or maybe it was her blood, her life force fighting, beating, screaming to be heard.

The power exploded in him. Her body surrendered a final jerk and tremble. He breathed deep, carefully relaxing his hold on her.

Her eyes stared up at the ceiling, the whites tinged pink, from lack of oxygen.

He sat back, sighing. "So pretty," he said yet again, caressing her face, her torso. Her pink polka-dotted bra cupped her young breasts. Too bad he couldn't get it up anymore. He would have loved to fuck her. Fuck her just as she took that last breath, as she gave up her essence. There was absolutely nothing, nothing in the world to match that moment of being buried deep inside a young woman just as she died and gave him her essence.

He shuddered at the thought.

Instead, he leaned over and kissed her one last time. "Thank you, special one."

Then, riding on the euphoria, he worked quickly, wrapping her in the plastic that lined the back of the van. Satisfied, he opened the side door. He had to stop what he was doing twice as cars, driving too fast on the road already slick with ice, curved into view. The tall, thick trees at least shadowed him partially. When it was clear, he tossed her shell away into the frozen ravine below. Between tonight's snowfall, the deep drifts already below, and the temps, she might never be found.

Elation zinged through him as he drove back down the mountain. The end was coming. He knew it. This one already left him feeling so, so strong.

Soon, he'd have the prize and then perhaps he could stop.

No, you won't.

At least he could stop for a while.

He smiled, the kiss, the kill, her essence fresh on his mind.

Chapter Ten

"Don't move," Max said yet again.

Lake sighed. "You know, this modeling gig was supposed to be fun." She stared up at the *latilla* ceiling like he wanted her to as the cool air whispered over her bare breasts. The antique fainting couch thing—probably had a very proper name, but damned if she knew it—was lumpy and uncomfortable as hell. A spring must be broken or something, she could swear it was poking her in the ass.

Max of course said nothing. She thought again of yesterday and how close they'd come to actually coming together, but hadn't. Which was probably a good thing, actually. Yes, it was, she knew it was, and yet...

And yet...

After that kiss, she wondered why the hell she had honest to God thought it would be better to wait, at least with Max. Well, she knew why, but it hardly mattered now, did it?

Anticipation and all that?

She almost rolled her eyes.

God the man was built. She knew what he tasted like, how he smelled just there where his neck met the rest of him. She'd followed that line with her tongue.

"Quit looking at me like that." He narrowed his eyes.

"Like what?" She grinned and batted her eyes at him.

"You're ruining my work."

"Can I see it?"

"No," he snapped and jabbed his brush into another glob of paint before slashing this way and that across the canvas.

What was he making a portrait of? Her? Her breasts? She was completely nude. The only time she'd ever been completely nude with a man, they had been doing something that wasn't art. Then again, she thought with a smile, maybe it had been. Though she wasn't completely bare. But gold gossamer strategically wrapped across the fronts of her breasts and down over her waist hardly counted as clothing in her opinion. Not when you could see through it. Transparent was the key word. Gossamer didn't keep out the cold or the wind.

An intent frown creased his brow as he narrowed his eyes even more, his jaw jutting out.

"You're sexy," she murmured.

"Dammit." His gray eyes flashed at her. "You know, I don't have a hell of a lot of time to paint, so when I do, I want to get done what I need to. My one day off and..."

She tried not to grin at the pissy artist emerging. "The muse and all that. Okay, I promise to try and be good."

He snorted, dipped his brush and started again. She refrained from asking how much longer, but honestly it was hard. She thought this would be fun, sexy, flirty. Here she was sexy and he was pissed she wouldn't be still so he could paint her. There was a boost to the ego. Not going there.

"Artists are strange sorts," she said.

He ignored her.

She sighed and tried to think of mundane things, but that just made her bored. Giving up, she focused on him and how intent he was, how focused on whatever it was he was painting.

His set, shadowed jaw flexed as though he was frustrated. Normally neat hair was slightly disarrayed from him running his fingers through it. The sleeveless denim shirt he wore was paint-splattered and obviously used for this very reason. Another side to him, how he worked, created.

She wanted him.

Mundane thoughts. Think of taxes. Inventory at the store.

Needing a distraction, she asked, "What is this called?"

"What?" he snapped.

"This couch thing, what is it called? Is it a fainting couch or—"

"Chaise." He cursed and she decided to be quiet. He was damned cute when he was aggravated.

Music softly played on the stereo. Something she'd never heard before but it was soothing, yet not. Low strummed guitars with a slight salsa flavor. Sexy music. There was no way she could look at him and not think what he didn't want her thinking. He was a great kisser...

Shaking her head, she closed her eyes and relaxed, breathed deep the scent of pine that always clung to Taos and now mixed with the stringent smell of turpentine and oil paints.

Slowly, she started to relax her muscles. She'd been tenser than she'd realized. Can't imagine why. Might have something to do with stress. Or unrelieved stress. Gee, could it be?

No, think nice thoughts. Easy thoughts. This room, the soft play of light across her body, the cool breeze that swished the silk hangings behind her.

Still he muttered, not loud enough that she could hear the words, but enough to know he was muttering. She wondered if he was as frustrated as she was.

Probably.

"You're doing it again," he whispered, his voice low and caressing.

"Doing what?" she asked, not opening her eyes.

"You know."

"Nope. No idea. Haven't a clue what the hell you're talking about."

Again he muttered, but she let herself relax and draw on that inner strength she'd questioned for so long, but knew in some part of her that she'd need soon. She'd need more than she'd ever needed anything before.

She'd been powerful once. Power could never be truly lost.

But she'd let someone strip her of that power.

She'd all but handed it over. Granted, she'd had years of self-doubt from her past to help it along, but she knew as well as anyone that only she could hand over her power. And she had.

She wanted it back, back like she used to have it, flowing through her.

Back so that she could look at someone and read them if she wanted to. Know if they were good or bad. If they were damaged or needed help. If they were healers or searching for healing themselves.

That she wanted back.

She imagined that power buried deep within her. Deep within her soul, locked away and protected. Maybe she hadn't exactly handed it over, but put it away. Something inside her clicked. Not given away, just *hidden*. Hiding from the bad people who could be out there. Who might be out there. She didn't want that. Didn't want them.

She wanted herself.

She found her.

A low lavender flame, edged in orange. That was *hers*. That was who she was. Focusing, she reached in and cupped the flame, imagined herself holding that precious gift, and blew slightly on it. As she nursed it, the flame grew, and grew, bursting out sparks so that she could see them fluming up to burst outwards, filling every corner of her soul, every fiber of her being.

The warmth flowed as her energy tingled through her system, renewing her, rejuvenating her sense of confidence. Her sense of self. Her sense of *power*.

Herself.

Lake gasped and opened her eyes.

"What the hell just happened?" Max asked, standing away from his easel, with a confused look on his face.

She blinked. "Umm...I don't know. Did I say something?"

His eyebrows rose. "No. No you didn't say anything, you almost looked like you weren't even breathing, then you sort of flushed and gasped." He ran his tongue around his teeth. "Fantasizing about me?"

She only grinned and shook her head.

"No?" He tapped his brush against the side of his thigh. "Really?"

A chuckle worked its way out. "Really. I promise."

She let it go at that as he went back to work on his painting.

But his aura...

God, before she thought she could feel it, but now?

Chills danced over her skin, flushed away by heat.

Where were her shields? Had she lost them?

Fear edged its way in, but she shoved it aside. This was different. She'd focus and she was focused on him. No wonder he was so clear. He was so clear she could see every color that shimmered and bled together. She could all but feel the waves of passion that swirled through the air only to be tempered with the cooler colors of logic, of reason. So analytical.

He glanced up and met her stare.

In his eyes was no malice. No evil. No anything but heat, passion, promise.

She licked her lips.

"You're doing that on purpose. Dammit."

She cocked an eyebrow at him, intent on telling him she wasn't doing anything other than reading his aura, but what came out was, "I'm scared."

He frowned. "What? Why? Of what?"

Lake sighed. How to explain this to him? "Never mind. I was just finding my inner strength. Sorry if that screwed your muse."

He studied her for a long moment, not moving, hardly even breathing. But his aura pulsed and tempted hers, reaching deep inside her to tickle within her belly. She shivered. Finally, one corner of his mouth edged up.

"Fine." With that, he picked up something that reminded her of paint sets.

Uh-oh.

"Uh...what are you..."

His eyes locked on her, moments ticking by, tension tightening her muscles. What was he thinking?

"You know me. There's nothing to be scared of." He still hadn't moved.

Maybe. Then again, maybe not.

Passion and desire thrummed off him in red and orange waves, purple swirling through them.

"You lost your chance in all this. All you had to do was be good and be still." He turned and sure enough it was a finger paint set. Finger paint? Next, he slowly poured a goblet of water.

She nibbled her lips, as something heated in her belly and it had nothing to do with her power.

He set the paints and the goblet of water beside her. His eyes narrowed as he unbuttoned the paint-splattered shirt.

She knew he was built because she'd watched him for months, felt his muscles as they'd rippled beneath her fingers last night.

But this?

Her breath caught.

Max might have a few gray hairs, but his body was one any woman between the ages of twelve and eighty-two would want.

He wasn't a bodybuilder by any means. No. The fact he kept in shape through various sports was clear in his muscular arms, the long torso with a well defined six pack. Trimmed, toned and so damn sexy her mouth watered just looking at him.

The man shouldn't be in better shape than she was.

Dark hair veed across his chest to trail down to the waist of his paint-speckled, ratty old jeans. She wanted to unbutton that fly and...

"Nuh-uh. Eyes on me," he said, his voice rough.

"Oh, they are." She licked her lips. "Believe me." She raised her gaze to his.

He gently cupped the side of her face in his hand. "No fear."

She sighed. "Fear is always waiting."

"No fear here, not between us." His thumb brushed back

133

and forth between her chin and ear. "You want this."

How did he do that? "You can read me way too easily."

She ran her hand over his chest, watching the way her light-skinned hand contrasted against his tanned muscles.

His dark chuckle caressed her. "I take it you like?"

She shifted and tucked her legs up under her, wrapping the useless gold gossamer around her. Might as well have been mosquito net. "How come you get to stay dressed and I don't?"

"It's better this way." His wicked grin tugged at her insides.

"Uh-huh."

Max sat beside her and dipped a finger in the goblet of water. She watched him. She couldn't *not* watch him.

That one-sided smile pulled at her gut. He glanced down and twirled the wet digit in dark purple paint.

Purple?

She leaned back as he moved towards her. "What are you doing?" She hadn't meant to whisper, but she did.

"Painting," he whispered back, coming even closer to kiss the tip of her nose. "Now close your eyes."

Instead she cocked an eyebrow at him.

"I've lots of scarves if you don't close them," he whispered, kissing her softly, then more insistently.

He moved to her neck.

"Scarves?" she asked.

"Blindfolds."

"I don't like—"

"Trust me," he whispered against her skin.

She opened her eyes and cupped his face in her hands. His stormy gray eyes held her stare. "I don't even know how to trust myself," she confessed.

The cool feel of his finger grazed up her arm. "Yes you do. You just need reminding. Now close your eyes."

For another minute, she looked into his eyes, searching, wondering and finally, conceding. Taking a deep breath, she closed her eyes.

"Now relax." His breath warmed the skin against the side of her neck before the heat of his mouth seared her. "And keep those gorgeous green eyes closed or I'll have to find my scarves." He licked her lips. "I think I have a purple one around here somewhere." He nipped her lips and she met his kiss. "No green. You need a green blindfold. It'll go great with your coloring."

He was talking about colors?

Strong fingers on her shoulders gently pushed her until she leaned against the back of the weird lounge-couch—chaise. He said it was a chaise.

Colors and furniture and—Oh God.

Cool wetness trailed from her shoulder, down over her chest to swirl around her breasts.

"What—" she started.

"Shhh." His mouth slanted insistently over hers, nibbling and nipping until she gave in.

She felt his smile against her mouth as he deepened the kiss. He tasted of coffee and cinnamon. The thick scent of oil paint and turpentine mixed with the spicy flavor that was all Max.

His fingers kept teasing, kept trailing cool wet paint over her skin. When he finally grazed across one nipple, she arched up and wrapped her arm around his neck. She bit his lip, sucking it deep then releasing it as he moved away.

One thigh moved between hers and again he patterned

paint across her chest and stomach.

Without thinking, she opened her eyes and met his gray stare. His smile, slightly amused, reminded her of a tiger that just realized his prey had fallen right into his lap.

Reaching behind her, he pulled out a long green strip of silk. He kept his gaze on hers as he leaned close again and pulled out another silk piece, this one purple. "You choose."

Her stomach flopped. "Oh, no. I promise I'll keep them…"

"Nope. You had your chance. No peeking. Keep them closed, I warned. You didn't listen, my Viking, now you have to pay the price." His deep voice rubbed across her nerves, teasing.

She blinked and, in that instant, she saw her own flame of power grow, felt the heat of it within her chest.

He breathed deep.

Reaching up, she grabbed the green. "This one."

Never taking his eyes from hers, he brushed the long strands of her hair behind her ears and then wrapped the silk across her eyes, carefully tying it so that it didn't pull her hair. His deft fingers were firm, yet gentle.

She hated to feel vulnerable.

"Now just lie back and relax."

"Right." But she tried.

This time, when he kissed her, when his chest pressed against hers, her breath stilled. The tickle of his chest hair, the warmth of his muscles. His hands cradled her face, his thumbs caressing the edge of the blindfold. His mouth devoured hers, and all she could think about was Max.

His scent, the other scents of the room assailed her.

The heat of his mouth contrasted with the coolness of his fingers. He kissed down her neck, grazed across her collarbone and twirled his tongue around her breast.

She moaned. She wanted all of his mouth on all of her.

"Tell me what you want," he whispered, his thigh coming between hers.

"I don't...I don't..." The gossamer whispered across her breasts, across her lower belly and she couldn't think.

"Then I'll just play until you figure it out." He chuckled. The material, soft as butterfly wings pulled tighter across her stomach.

His hands were busy everywhere. Trailing over her arms. She could feel the chilled trails of paint, contrasting with the heat of his touch as his fingers, his palms, caressed her. Over her stomach, across her hipbones until she squirmed.

"A soft spot," he whispered, his voice gruff, as he kissed his way down her body. "I love finding those."

She wanted to touch him. Reaching out, she settled her hands on his shoulders. Then he stopped. "I have another idea. Give me your hand."

She frowned.

"It'll be better, you know it will." He whispered against her lips.

Lake swallowed.

He placed a piece of silk in her hand. Then gently took her other hand and placed it on the other end of the silk. "Now stretch out."

She turned her head towards his voice and shifted so that she was more reclining.

"Now put your hands above your head."

She hesitated.

"Lake. I'm not going to tie you up, for crying out loud. We'll try that another time. Today, I just want you to hold on to the silk in both hands."

This she could do. Taking a deep breath, she followed his instructions. In her mind, she could see how she must look, blindfolded, her arms stretched above her head so that her breasts were on display for him. Her breasts? Hell, her whole body.

Max looked down at the work of art before him. And she was that, a fine, beautiful, luscious work of art. He dipped his fingers in the cool water, wiping the extra paint that remained on his jeans.

"You're beautiful." He ran his hand from her wrist down her arms, over her paint-patterned chest, over her stomach. "Some day I'm going to paint you just like this."

He trailed his fingers across her hip bones, noticed how she jerked at the movement. He smiled. The gossamer was an interesting touch. He kept up the movements of his hands, noticing the contrast from his tanned, paint-splattered hand against the paleness of her skin.

The gold material...

Watching her face, he ran his hand up under her leg and lifted it, bending it at the knee. With the other hand, he took the end of the fabric and looped it between her thighs, tucking it up under her.

"What—"

He leaned over and kissed her, kissed her as he wanted to for the rest of his days. She tasted of secrets, of something that was only Lake. Her scent filled his nostrils and all he wanted was her.

But he didn't want to rush. He didn't want a quick fuck.

He wanted to cherish. To seduce. To enjoy.

This time, he followed his hands with his mouth. He played

with her breasts, twirling, caressing, tweaking until she writhed against him, her breath coming faster. "Stop playing and get on with it."

"But I like to play." He kissed his way down her stomach. Instead of moving the thin gossamer out of his way, he kissed her through it. Soaking the fabric with his tongue. He twirled over her navel and moved lower.

The thin strip of hair covering her mound matched the dark red of her hair. He grinned as he eased her thighs apart. Knowing what she wanted, he kissed his way down each leg, running his hands up her inner thighs.

"Dammit, Max. Please..." She shifted on the couch and he smiled.

She spread her legs, giving him a view he wouldn't forget any time soon. He traced circular patterns over her inner thighs, closer and closer, watching her reactions...

So responsive.

Lake wanted to reach out and touch him. But then he might stop... Instead she pulled on the material between her hands.

She jumped as his tongue, hot and wet, licked the inside of her thigh. Please...

Then his fingers circled higher and higher until finally, they touched her. She jerked at the first caress.

"Somebody is having fun," his deep voice whispered. The heat of his breath against her sent chills dancing over her skin.

The soft material shifted against her yet again, rubbing across that bundle of nerves and she just wanted...

He kissed her, his fingers and his tongue making her forget who the hell she was. She wanted more.

The gossamer pulled tighter across her, and she jerked

harder on the silk. His mouth, or her essence, soaked the fabric between her thighs even as it rubbed across that one spot that would... She couldn't keep her moans locked in any more. His mouth was wicked, his tongue hot, his fingers fast, light, then harder until she couldn't think, couldn't reason, all she could do was feel.

Behind her eyelids, colors burst, sparked. Her purple flame teased bigger, hotter, brighter. She wanted that.

Fire licked through her veins, burning in her soul.

His tongue danced up and down her, from side to side through the material.

"Oh God, Max! Max!"

She was going to come and he hadn't even entered her.

"Let go," he whispered.

He twirled his tongue gently, lightly over her clit and she was lost.

Fire shot through her, from her center outwards to her fingertips.

She shivered, shook and moaned. And still he kept kissing her, kept licking her, kept playing over her, his fingers slick with her essence. Yet never once had he entered her.

Max kissed her one last time, the taste of her heady on his tongue. He wanted more. He wanted her.

Leaning up, he ripped the gossamer material away and watched as still she trembled. For him. What he could give her.

She'd surrendered. He unbuttoned his fly and shucked his jeans, grabbing the condom from the pocket. He'd hoped, hadn't really planned this, but God, he'd hoped.

This time, he didn't seduce her. He fisted his hand on himself as he rolled the latex on.

Kneeling on the lounge between her thighs, he realized he'd

never wanted a woman as much as he wanted this one.

"We're not done yet," he told her, looking down where she still glistened. He moved forward, until he could feel the heat of her against him. He wasn't going to last long.

"God, I hope not!" she said, looping her arms around him and jerking him down for a kiss. Her mouth was hot, her tongue licking his lips. He knew she could taste herself on him.

He took a deep breath and ripped the blindfold off her. Her green eyes were even brighter than usual. "Not even close to being done," he promised.

She cradled him between her thighs. He reached down, parted her, and gritted his teeth as he trembled. Her wetness coated his fingers and he rimmed her slick passage once, twice before he couldn't take it anymore.

He guided himself to her opening.

Her eyes closed.

"No. Look at me." Her heat closed over him, gripping him like a fist.

Her eyes locked with his and he couldn't look away as he slowly sank inch by inch into her.

"Yes." She shuddered on a moan and leaned her head back, giving him her neck.

"You feel so damned good."

"Max."

He was lost. Lost in a sensation of her. He kissed her, her mouth hot and demanding on his. Her legs came up around him, her heels locking into the small of his back.

He pulled almost all the way out, then sank slowly back in.

She moaned and moved with him, against him, urging him on. Their lovemaking deepened. He had no idea when it happened, but he sensed it all the way to the very center of him.

Some part of her mixed with some part of him, and not just down where they joined. He opened his eyes to see her watching him. Colors danced around them, through them, on them.

Max bit down and stroked her faster. Deeper. Harder.

He felt her trembling, knew she was almost there.

Heat built low in his back, tightened his balls.

"Max! Max!"

"That's it. Now, Lake."

Her inner muscles squeezed around him, jerking him headlong into the hardest orgasm of his life. Stars exploded behind his eyelids, as she bowed up in his arms, she yelled his name.

All he could feel was Lake.

All he could hear was Lake.

All there was for him, was Lake.

Chapter Eleven

Max lay there. He was breathing—at least he thought he was.

"Are we alive?"

"No." Her neck was warm. He nuzzled the soft skin and grinned when she squirmed. "Another soft spot."

Unfortunately he had no energy left to do anything about it.

Her legs slid off his back. They lay half on the chaise lounge. Cursing, he went ahead and pulled them both to the floor. The paints lay to the side and the goblet tipped over and spread a puddle of water across the drop cloth.

He didn't really care.

"Colors," she muttered, kissing his jaw. "I saw the rainbow."

He grinned and turned so that she was lying tucked to his side. "The rainbow?"

"Mmm. All the colors. Yours. Mine. Mixing. Melding."

He hadn't imagined it then. He tried to catch his breath. "Melding. I remember something like us melding."

She snorted, cuddling against him.

He closed his eyes and rubbed her arm, dry paint crackling and flaking off under his fingers. Grinning, he leaned up on his elbow and looked down at her.

Purple paint patterns swirled up her arms, across her breasts to ring her nipples.

She opened her eyes and glanced down at herself. "Finger painting has taken on a whole new meaning."

"Has it?"

She glanced at him from under her lashes. He traced her pale red brows, perfectly arched, and realized she had freckles across her skin.

"Freckles. I've always had a soft spot for freckles." He leaned over and kissed her shoulder.

"Will this paint come off?"

He laughed. "It's not henna, or stain."

Her brows rose.

"Yes. It will come off."

"One of these days I get to paint you."

He traced the line of her nose, then leaned over and kissed the bridge. "Promise?"

"With green finger paint." She nipped his lip and squirmed out from under him. "Then you can look like a leprechaun."

He sat up, since she obviously was full of energy. She stood in the sunlight and stretched. He loved simply watching her, the way she moved, the grace, the ease. Hell, the way the sunlight burned in her hair.

"Beautiful," he whispered, sitting up. There wasn't a shy bone in her body. *Thank you.*

She tossed her long red hair over her shoulder and looked at him. "You just want me again."

He laughed and pulled himself to his feet. "Mmmm."

She picked at the paint, winced. "Shower?"

He tugged her to him and kissed her. "No. I've a better

idea."

She leaned into him and kissed him back, her naked body fitting perfectly with his. "You're just full of ideas, aren't you?" She nibbled his lip. "It doesn't have anything to do with paint does it?"

"Hmm. It could." He led her down the hallway to the living apartments.

She slowed. "You know, we probably shouldn't be traipsing about naked."

"Don't worry. Alyssa went to Santa Fe to shop. So we can currently traipse, naked or otherwise." He glanced at her as he led her back to his bedroom and into the master bath. "Naked is my choice. Naked is beautiful."

"So says a guy with a perfect body."

He grinned. "You like my body?"

She rolled her eyes. "Like you couldn't tell?"

She liked his body. "I guess flexing my muscles would not win me any points?"

Her smile made him think of all the things he really wanted to do to—and with—her mouth.

"That," she said, running her hand over his chest, down to his groin to grip him, "would depend on which muscles you want to flex."

He sucked in a breath but pushed her hand away.

She glanced around at his dark tiled bathroom. "Ohhhh, I want your shower." The shower was free standing in the corner of the bathroom. Three jets came out at various points. He turned her instead to the deep Jacuzzi tub in the opposite corner.

"But I want you in the Jacuzzi."

She laughed and leaned back against him. "That works

145

too."

He turned on the tub and they played, laughing and exploring while the water steamed up the room.

The thought that she belonged here, with him, in this house, flirted unbidden into his mind.

"I wonder if the colors will come back," she murmured, her skin all but glowing.

"I don't know," he stood behind her, running his hands over her fantastic body, all curves and valleys. She squirmed.

"You are so damned sexy," he whispered, gently moving her hair aside to kiss the nape of her neck.

"You're more athletic than I am."

"What?" he pulled back.

"Nothing."

He walked them to the mirror.

She blinked and then laughed. "I look like a deranged artist played with me."

Her laughter danced over him as he cupped her luscious breasts. "So he did, but you know what I see?"

"A masterpiece?" she quipped, shoving a long red strand of hair out of her way.

"And then some."

"I was joking."

He met her gaze in the mirror. "I'm not. You're beautiful. Exquisite. A real woman."

She arched a brow at him. "If that's what you see, I won't shatter your illusions."

"You don't think you're beautiful?" he asked. He'd just have to show her otherwise, but then he liked goals.

She sighed, narrowed her gaze. "Oh, I *know* I'm beautiful

and I've used that knowledge. But I also know that my body is not what appeals to every man." She turned one way and then the other looking in the mirror. "A little too...too..." She scrunched up her nose. "Un-toned."

"Un-toned? That's not a word."

"In my beautiful world it is."

"You're perfect." His arms tightened around her. "And thank God you don't appeal to every man. I don't want *every* man lusting after you. I'd go out of my mind then."

She laughed and turned in his arms. "Out of your mind? And why is that?"

"Oh, well, I guess I'm turning out to be the jealous type."

Her hands kept moving over him, her nails softly scraping over his skin. "I never really liked the jealous type before."

"New things for the both of us, my Viking goddess."

She snorted and kissed him. "Delusional and jealous," she whispered against his mouth. "Those can be seen as not very healthy qualities."

He seduced her mouth with his lips, her body with his hands. "That's okay. I've got therapy."

"Really?" she asked, arching against him.

"Yep. Creative." He cupped her bottom, trailing his fingers lower until he parted her, the warmth of her desire coating his fingers. She shuddered as he traced her. "And physically active."

She laughed and pulled him over to the tub. He picked up the remote and clicked the jets on, another button and music filled the room. She twisted her hair up, and looked around his bathroom, finally picking up a couple of paintbrushes that she found standing in an empty vase beneath the mirror. She shoved them into the mass of hair to keep it up on her head.

She climbed in first, but when he started to slide into the water, she stopped him and pushed him onto the wide tiled lip that circled the inset tub.

Her eyes twinkled with amusement and darkened with passion. "Therapy is important." She leaned over and kissed him, moving down to bite on his neck. "We wouldn't want you to have any negative issues arise because you didn't get enough..." She met his gaze as she lowered herself into the water and moved between his thighs.

"Enough?" he asked, though not really following the conversation. "Oh, therapy."

He ran his fingers over her hair, cupping her cheek, his thumb moving back and forth over her plump bottom lip.

She kissed his thigh, then licked, kissed, and nibbled a trail right to where he wanted her. Her eyes never left his and he gripped the edge of the tub to keep from grabbing her.

Her hands stole his breath as she grazed up and down his shaft with her nails, then her lips, until finally, *finally*, she put her mouth on him. He wanted to watch her, but his eyes slid closed on the exquisite feeling of her hot wet mouth moving on him, around him. When her lips closed over the head of his cock, he hissed. The twirl of her tongue pulled a moan from him. But then she started to move, to suck, and he lost all train of thought. Her hands...wicked. He couldn't follow her movements, her hands, her mouth. It all rolled together to rip a growl from him, until he gripped her head between his hands.

She let him go with a pop. "Nuh-huh. It's your turn. No touching. Keep your hands on the edge."

He frowned at her.

One russet brow rose. "Would you like me to get out and go find a scarf?" Her eyes looked towards his closet. "Though I'm sure a tie would work too."

Taking a deep breath, he sucked air into his burning lungs and fisted his hands on the edge of the tile. The water swirled around them. Steam rose to slick her skin with a light sheen of moisture.

He wanted to lick it all off her.

Instead he focused on those gorgeous breasts of hers bobbing in the water.

She moved again, closer to him, nestling between his legs.

He closed his eyes and then opened them, watching as she moved closer and closer, but never touching.

"Don't tease," he told her.

"Or?"

This time he grinned. "Oh, you'll find out."

For a long minute she held his gaze, then whispered against him. "I'll try that another time. Right now, what I want is right here."

Max could do nothing other than watch as her mouth closed over him. This time there was no teasing, no easing nibbles or kisses to build up...

She sucked him deep and he groaned, his hips lifting of their own volition.

"Lake," he growled.

She didn't stop, didn't slow, but sucked him harder, deeper, her hands busy at the base of his shaft and balls.

He tried to hold on, to make it last, but hell, he'd been fantasizing about that mouth of hers for months.

Max wanted inside her. Now. But he couldn't. He should...

Her hands did something and her mouth did something else and he was fucking lost.

His release tore through him. He bowed up, shouting.

Vaguely, he realized she was still moving on him, her mouth milking every last drop from him, her hands on his hips.

He dropped his head to his chest and gripped her head. Holding her stare, he jerked the brushes free, smiling as her hair rioted around her shoulders, the ends floating in the water. He ran his fingers through the silky red tresses.

Finally, she let him go, licking the last of his passion from him.

Her smile pulled at his gut and he wanted her again. "I can't feel my fingers. Or my feet. Or hell," he sighed, sliding down into the water, "even my head."

She twirled a finger around the head of his cock.

"Not that head."

Laughing, she moved to sit beside him, but he didn't let her. Instead, he pulled her astride him and jerked her to him for a kiss.

"I'm going to have you so hot, so ready, you'll beg me," he warned her. "And then, I'll make you beg me more."

"Promises, promises." She moved her head to the side as he kissed down her neck, cupping her breasts.

"You better damned well believe it."

Chapter Twelve

Alyssa sat at a table near the back of the coffee shop, brochures and books scattered around her. It was late afternoon, the sun already sinking low in the sky. She'd been back from Santa Fe for only half an hour but had the feeling she just shouldn't go home yet. Not quite yet. She glanced across the street and noticed colors still danced out of the windows of the loft apartment.

She smiled. About time Dad and Lake got on with it.

Shaking off the thoughts, she focused back on her current project—college. College? What to do? Where to go? Which direction to head? She really hated decisions like this. How the hell was she supposed to *know* what she wanted to do with the rest of her life?

For now, she was happy she was figuring out the here and now, forget the forever future, which really wasn't forever anyway, was it?

The now was more important to her than the future that may or may not happen. Life could end very quickly. So for the now? Now she'd rather be reading one of the new books in her bag she'd purchased in Santa Fe. Books on shielding and proper health for psychics. Not that she'd start eating tofu. Tofu was, in her opinion, gross. Yogurt she could handle. Greens and alfalfa sprouts, fine. Fish and grilled veggies—yeah. Tofu, no. So the chapter on no meats was going to be a waste. Plus she'd seen the way Lake ate and Alyssa would bet that woman didn't read books on the proper diet of a psychic. Who did these people think they were anyway?

And who was dumber, the author thinking she had so much important information to impart, or the idiot who bought the book? Still, there might be something good in here. If nothing else than the chapter on the importance of sleep patterns and protecting herself when she could be vulnerable. Things stole into the psyche when one was vulnerable. Nightmares were a perfect example. And things waited for vulnerability in sleep. It was classic, and for her, a time to worry about.

Sleep. Shields. Vulnerability. Nightmares. Visions.

Hell. She rubbed her face.

Last night had been a bad one. She'd dreamed the monster with the red daggers was choking her and nothing she could do would stop it. Then she'd heard Lake's voice and her dad's, and something had burst inside her and the dark monster with the red eyes suddenly vanished. Not sure what the hell it meant, but then she was stressed about the darkness she couldn't find.

This was why so many people thought she was certifiable. Looking for something she couldn't find? Darkness?

But she *knew* it was real. There was no doubt in her mind about that any more. In the last few weeks she'd come to believe. Really believe. She was real. Her gift was real. The lurking evil she couldn't readily see, that was real. Why couldn't she readily see it? Propping her chin on her hand, she stared at the stuff on the table and wondered when exactly she'd started to accept herself the way she was. There wasn't any one moment, she realized. It had just sorta started to happen and kept happening.

"Whatchya working on back here?" Mark asked, sliding into the chair across from her. He picked up the book and grinned. "*The Healthy Psychic?*"

Instead of answering, she jerked it away.

"You never cease to amaze, Lys."

"Then I'm on track."

Shaking his head, he picked up a brochure on the graphic arts program from the Art Institute of Dallas. "I thought you were going to take classes here in Taos?" He flipped through it.

"Well, I'm leaving my options open. I probably will do just that, but does that mean I can't also take some online courses that might help me out in the long run? I thought I'd take the web graphics program here to get a more hands-on experience with the scripting that's so important now. I don't understand Java or even Flash and I want to. Plus here I can get experience with Quark and a few other programs, right?"

Mark leaned onto his fist and nodded. "Yeah, you can do all that here. And it is nice to have a professor or a lab partner to help you out if you don't understand what is going on."

She tapped the red and white brochure. "But I want to take the advanced digital graphics courses through them. I'm hoping to get into the summer program here and either the fall or the next winter session with the Art Institute Online thing. I figure I can use the graphics design part, but I want to *know* the website stuff inside and out. Because there are good websites out there and those that, well..."

"Suck," Mark said, grinning at her.

She smiled back. "Yeah, and if not for you, I probably wouldn't have thought of all this. But now that I've played with it, I like it and think it's probably something that I'd want to do, ya know?"

"Versus what else you might like to do?"

"Well, there isn't anything else I'd like to do. I've always loved art."

"Can't imagine where that came from."

She shoved his arm out from under him. "But I've a feeling my paintings, which are more therapy, are not works of art that will appeal to most."

"But they might." He shrugged. "Don't close off your options."

She thought about that. About the fact that her father gave her the privacy and space she needed when she wanted to paint, but also liked to see her work. Whether it was the act of a concerned parent, or the pride thing, she wasn't sure. Probably both. But he never invaded her work. He always waited until she asked for his opinion. The man did run a gallery. The last conversation brought a smile to her face.

"Yeah, well, Dad wants me to think about doing a showing. If and when I'm ready."

He nodded. "That's great."

"Maybe. Or maybe it's because he missed having any of my drawings and artwork to put on a fridge."

"And his gallery is like a giant magnet board to proudly display his daughter's work."

"Could be."

"Please, don't be stupid." Mark leaned closer. "Your father doesn't have the time or the patience for pity showings."

True. So maybe she would think about it.

"There are worse things than being an artist, Alyssa."

She nodded. "True, I just don't like that starving part. So I want a profession that will bring me the things I need."

"Like food and shelter."

"Exactly." She laughed.

For a minute they just stared at each other. Then he said, "You're really pretty, you know that?"

She blinked. Mark thought she was pretty? She blinked again wondering if she was hallucinating.

He coughed. "I mean..."

Alyssa glanced up as someone stopped at their table. Thad. And he was glaring at his brother. Great. He slapped his hand on Mark's shoulder. "Little bro. Give it up. She's taken. Plus, you don't seem to really have the knack."

Mark didn't even look at his brother—his eyes stayed on Alyssa.

Thad's over-possessiveness lately really grated on her. One thing she had learned and totally agreed with was that she needed to be her own person, set her own boundaries, learn her own self-worth before venturing forth to give it to anyone else, if she so chose.

Which she currently did not.

And certainly not with Thad.

"Thad," she said, propping her chin on her fist, "what makes you think I'm taken?"

Thad leaned over the table between her and Mark. "'Cause I know you, babe."

She didn't answer. Instead she only looked at him until he finally blinked and looked away.

"First off," she started, "I'm not taken, and if I were, it wouldn't be with the likes of you."

"Ohhhh." Mark laughed. "Crash and burn. What was that you were saying, bro?"

"Shut up," Thad said, straightening. He tried to grin at her, but instead of charming, she found it annoying. Annoying and irritating.

"You know, Thad, you should try to charm the ladies somewhere else. I'm working and was trying to have a conversation here."

"About what?" He picked up the brochures. "School? Cool. You're going to Dallas?" His blue gaze swung back to her. "Sweets, we could have all sorts of fun in the big D."

She shook her head. "Thad. There's no *we* and that's an online school."

"But it doesn't have to be."

"But it is." She finally just punched his shoulder. "Quit being such an ass, Thad. It's beneath you. And it's making your aura shift into an ugly color."

Mark laughed and Thad finally grinned at her. "Maybe so, but you gotta know which brother is better, don't you?"

"Nah, I've already figured that one out." She waggled her brows at him. "Besides, you just don't kiss as well as Mark."

Why she said that, she had no idea, but she did and there it was. Even if she had absolutely no idea how Mark kissed.

Shock was the first thing she noticed on his face. Clear, unadulterated shock. Poor guy.

Mark stopped laughing.

"When the hell did you kiss her?" Thad asked, whirling on his brother. "I asked you if you liked her and you said no. You said she was all free and clear to choose whomever she wanted."

And why were they talking about her as if she wasn't here?

Mark opened his mouth, closed it, then opened it again, his eyes big on her. She took pity on him.

"Mark's so sweet, he'd never kiss and tell." She scooted her chair closer to Mark. "Unlike some people I know."

Thad looked from one to the other. "Is this a joke?"

She paused, took a deep breath and then dropped the shields she'd carefully spent the morning building. Anger waved off of him, hot and pulsing. "Why are you mad?"

He only blinked at her and then sat in the last chair at the small table. "Hell if I know. I've asked you out I don't know how many times for dates. We even went out a few."

"We occasionally hung out, Thad." She patted his hand. "We never dated."

He shrugged. "Maybe I wanted more."

She remembered and this was really why she'd never let them get closer, another reason she hadn't wanted anything serious with him. "Yes, I know, and I had fun." Sighing, she patted his hand. "And you do kiss really well. But you're not ready for more."

He rolled his eyes. "My brother lied."

She smiled. "Maybe. But then again, it doesn't matter if he wanted me or not, or if you did or not. It's me. I choose. You. Him. Someone else."

One blond brow arched. "Yeah, I get that."

"No woman likes to be a bone between two dogs."

Mark shifted. "I never—"

She held up her hand. "I know, Mark."

"You do?"

This time, she laughed as she packed her stuff up. Thad was still sullen as he stared at her. "You sure you don't want to run off to Dallas with me?"

She shook her head and shoved the books into her bag. "No. I'd probably kill you before we even reached the state line."

"I doubt that. Why would you do that?" He crossed his hands over his chest. "I'm the epitome of charm, my lady."

Alyssa just wanted out of here. "Charm and smarm."

"Ouch."

The two brothers might look alike, but they were as different as night and day. Once upon a time she would have gone for Thad. Those days were over. Now she found that Mark's quiet, friendly way was more her style. Maybe. Maybe not.

"I thought you two were just friends," Thad said.

She huffed and swung her pack on her back. "And what? We can't be friends with benefits?" She turned and walked away.

Thad's furious whisper made her smile. "Her father is gonna fucking kill you."

Yeah, well, she didn't think that would happen. Maybe, but then again, she was tired of Thad's crap. Maybe now he'd leave her alone.

One little white lie.

Of course she might have made more trouble for Mark. Glancing back over her shoulder, she noticed the guy had the biggest smile on his face she'd ever seen.

Figured.

Men were idiots.

He watched her on the street, wondering which way she would go. She looked up at her father's apartments. Probably not going over there any time soon. He too glanced over to see the unlit windows, though he felt like he should be able to see something. To see, to know what was happening there. At least in terms of powers and emotions.

Instead...

He focused on the windows and for just a moment, just a brief moment, saw a swirl of orange and red.

Passion.

From Lake, he was sure.

Taking a deep breath, he turned his attention back to the one he wanted. The one who would boost his life longer than all the others had. Who would, if he was lucky, heal him.

Part of him, some part of him wondered, what if she wasn't the last one? What if he needed another? Then what would he do?

Already he was weak. He'd have to move fast. The last one had taken him too long to finish. Her essence and life force had charged him, but only for a little while.

The charges were shorter and shorter.

This one had to heal him.

She was so damned powerful.

And he wondered if she knew.

He saw her glance back into the coffee shop, the frown on her face to be replaced by a smile as she shook her head.

He breathed deep, the cold air slicing his lungs, slicing through his clothing. Always fucking cold. He was always cold.

A headache pulsed deep today. He would not have much time.

Tick.

Tick.

Tick.

It had to be now. Had to be.

He *knew* it.

Closing his eyes, he could swear he smelled her scent

dancing with the smell of the snow from the mountains. It would be cold tonight. He glanced up to Taos peak. The snowfall up there was heavier than he thought, all but obscuring the bottom half of the mountains.

The skiers would be happy. The resort even happier. The snow would help. He wondered if it would move into the valley tonight. He hadn't checked the weather. At least the body he'd dumped would be covered even more. With luck it would be several weeks yet before they found her, and by then the animals would have gotten to her.

The memory of what that young woman had felt like as she died danced through his mind, heating his blood, making him want this one even more.

She paused and looked around as if she sensed him.

He'd have to be more careful. The sickness had weakened more than just his body. He needed to focus.

Didn't want her to feel him, to *find* him before he'd even gotten to her.

He had to get to her, to capture her. To have her.

Shielding, he followed not too closely, but close enough. She wasn't in a hurry. She waved to several people, said hello to others and stopped and chatted with the Dancing Moon shop owner. The store's eclectic clothing hung from the eaves outside its door and danced in the icy evening breeze.

He watched as the women spoke. He'd always liked the way her hands moved when she talked. She ran her hand through her hair and smiled at the shop owner.

People were drawn to her, even as she tried to remain distant. He'd seen that the first time he'd met her. She was a soul whom others liked, respected and wanted to be around.

There were not many of those in the world. At least not with her gifts and abilities.

160

She was perfect. She'd always been perfect. He should have taken her first and been done with it, but he thought perhaps he had been wrong. He'd hoped she wasn't really for him, but the feeling inside, that he needed her, had only grown. He'd tried to shove it aside because he liked Alyssa.

But...

Things changed.

She might be powerful, but she was still so new, so...raw. He grinned. It would have been fun to train her, but he didn't have that kind of time. And that was hardly what he needed her for. What he needed from her was something that had to be taken, that could not be learned, couldn't be expanded on.

Once upon a time, he would have let her live.

But not now.

He waited until she moved along with a group of people spilling out of one of the restaurants.

He smiled, knowing where she was going. He checked his watch. It wasn't six yet. Not quite.

Six was when the bookstore closed. And though she'd been gone all day and the books peeking out of her bag told him she'd bought more somewhere else, he knew she'd go to the familiar. People were so predictable.

Smiling to himself, he slipped away and planned. He knew he'd have to be careful. Her father would raise holy hell and then some.

There was also the woman now. The woman spending time with Alyssa. Powerful enough to teach a novice. And if she'd known what Alyssa was, then she had to be powerful as well.

Maybe, maybe he'd take them both.

The thought had merit.

He just had to get Alyssa first.

❧

Alyssa's phone rang and she waved to the owner of the Dancing Moon, who was taking down the dresses, and answered it.

"Hello?"

"Um, is this Alyssa? From the gallery?"

She paused, thought about the voice. And his face rose in her mind. Wire-rimmed glasses and intense eyes. "Yes."

"This is Jonathan Murbanks. You guys will be showcasing my work." *I hope* was unsaid, yet she heard it all the same.

She remembered his aura, the way it had shimmered, the edges melding with hers so that for a minute when she met him, she couldn't think, couldn't remember what the hell she'd walked into the studio for.

It had been several days ago.

He'd smelled really good. Expensive cologne, not too sweet, nor too spicy, some perfect balance in between. Simple, classic with just a hint of flavor. Like his photos.

"Yes," she said. "I remember you, Mr. Murbanks."

"Oh. You do?"

She smiled. "Yeah. I've been going over which photos we're going to display and what size we're going to print them in."

It had been hard to get the young artist out of her mind. Then again, he wasn't that young. He was older than her, but thanks to Dad, she thought of him as *that young artist.* Or just *Murbanks.* Dad always said it with a hint of something in his voice.

But she couldn't help but think of him. She tried not to.

The day they'd met and she'd walked into the gallery, either she had stopped or the world had. When she'd walked in and seen him, seen the way his aura had reached out and touched hers, she simply couldn't *not* stop. She'd tried to shove it away. After all, she really didn't have the time for a guy.

Not that he wanted her to have the time—

"...this weekend." He stopped.

Shit. What had he been saying?

"I'm sorry, Jonathan. I lost you for a minute. What did you say?"

She heard him take a deep breath. "I was wondering if you were busy this weekend. Or tomorrow evening? Or this evening?"

Alyssa laughed, pleasure surging through her. Why, she'd think about later. "Umm."

"I mean, if you're busy, I understand. Or if you just don't want to, I get that too."

She smiled and continued to walk towards the bookstore. "If I don't want to what?"

"Oh." He laughed. "I promise I'm not an idiot, or then again, maybe I am. I just saw you and something..." He sighed. "Anyway, I'd love to take you out. Dinner. Lunch. Coffee. Hell, skiing."

Skiing, it had been a while since she'd skied, been even longer since she'd boarded. Those days were over.

"I don't ski anymore," she confessed. "My knees were damaged."

"Oh, I'm sorry."

"So am I. I miss skiing." She stepped around a couple walking too slow and whispering to each other. "But the resort is still a good place to hang. If you don't mind a short drive, so's

Red River and Angel Fire. Both are also good places." And why the hell was she rambling?

She glanced over her shoulder at the couple and smiled. Maybe there was such a thing as love. Or at least the hope of it. Her dad seemed happy lately. Tense, but happy. And Lake smiled more. She assumed love, that elusive thing was out there.

Just because her mom had been too difficult to live with did not mean that there wasn't love out there. Not that she wanted love, but it was nice to know it was there...if she wanted it.

She realized he hadn't said anything. Great, rambling girl scares off interested and interesting artist.

"Hello?" she asked.

For a minute he didn't say anything. "Coffee would be good."

"Great. When?"

Earnest and eager. She was tired, yet happy.

"Tonight?" he pressed.

She smiled to herself.

"Are you smiling?" he asked.

She stopped and looked around, wondering how he knew. "I am."

And then again, she was certifiable. A slew of pysch docs had told her so. "Maybe," she said.

"You are. I know."

"You know?" She started towards the bookstore again, shaking off the uneasiness. "How do you know?"

He sighed. "Would it freak you out if I said sometimes I just know things, or rather feel them?"

"Maybe."

"From the girl who said my aura was interesting?"

She chuckled. "Touché." She stepped off the curb and crossed the street, heading between the two buildings and the alley. "So you're an empath?"

"And if I were?"

"I'd ask how much of one you are." She focused on his voice and tried to read him, tried to feel him. Within a blink, she simply did. Holy shit. She could feel his desire, his happiness and ... "Never mind."

"You do anything other than auras?" he asked.

She could only laugh. "Maybe we should save something for our...coffee?"

"How about dinner too?"

"Let's see how coffee goes."

"In an hour?" he asked.

She checked her watch and saw she only had about ten minutes before the shop closed. That should give her enough time to check Yancey's books before going home to clean up. Or enough time to call home first to warn Dad she was coming home to clean up. She'd just leave out the part that she was seeing Murbanks.

"Works for me."

"See you then."

"Yeah, see you."

When she cut the call off, she shielded up again. He could read her, over the phone? Was he that good or was it just that they connected? She'd have to ask Lake.

Holy crap, she had a date.

A d-a-t-e. Or would that be D-A-T-E? Not that she'd never

had one. No matter what she'd said to Thad, she knew they had gone on dates, little nothings. But they had never felt like this. She was freaking. She'd always wondered what people meant when they talked about butterflies in the stomach. She'd been nervous before recitals, or plays in school, but never really with a guy. Never like this. Butterflies? Felt more like a group of small birds was bouncing around in her stomach.

Deep breath. Maybe she needed to take up yoga.

What the hell was she going to wear? Oh my God, she had a date. Panic skittered through her nerves. No, not *really* a date. It was coffee. Just coffee. Right? With the possibility of dinner, with a guy who was older. Who found her interesting and not in a freaky way. A guy who was an empath.

A date.

She smiled. It was going to be okay.

She decided she'd call and warn Dad now so by the time she got there, it wouldn't be weird. Or at least not *too* weird.

She hit "one" on her phone and speed-dialed her father. The thought that she was nineteen and should have another number one flitted through her brain, as it always did when she dialed it. But it was what it was. Her dad was, actually, pretty cool. It rang and she waited while the machine picked up. "Dad, it's me, I just wanted you to know I'm going to be home in about fifteen minutes after I get the Grimm Brothers to order this book I want." Taking a deep breath and wondering why she was so nervous, she hurried on, "I've got to get ready." She smiled. "I've got a date."

Deciding not to tell him who it was with, she hung up. She shoved the door, since it was usually stuck, into the bookstore. Like always, it squeaked as she opened it.

Jay was behind the counter today and she paused. She could drop her shields and read things, but then she'd weird out and want to leave before she asked them to order her book. She'd seen one she wanted today in Santa Fe but she didn't want to pay fifty bucks for it. So she'd have Yancey order a used copy for her.

Or that was her plan until she walked in.

Jay.

Sighing, she smiled and leaned onto the counter. "Hi. Is Yancey in?"

Jay looked pale again and skinnier, if that was possible. He rubbed a hand over his face and looked at her from under his brows. His yellow eyes danced over her nerves.

Should just come back tomorrow.

"I can h-h-help you."

She shouldn't be rude, but she really wanted to get out of here.

"I'm sure you can." She sighed. What the hell. She'd just order the book and get out of here.

"There you are!" Yancey said. "I was wondering when we'd see you again. I had a feeling you'd be in."

She grinned at him. "And so I am."

Jay started to get off the stool behind the counter, but Yancey put a hand on his arm. "You can help her, Jay. Just ask her what she needs."

Jay frowned. "W-wh-what do you need?"

She took out a piece of paper with the title and author on it. "I was wondering if you guys could order this book for me."

Yancey laughed and patted her hand. "I'm sure we can, Alyssa." He turned to his brother. "Jay, you look this up on the computer like I showed you, and we'll see if we can get it for our Alyssa." Then he turned back to her. "Would you like some of that passion tea you like?"

She started to say no, but realized she was thirsty. She agreed and waited.

Yancey returned in a couple of minutes with a steaming cup of tea in a blue mug and handed it to her. "Did you find it, Jay?"

Jay nodded. "There's three editions, which do you want?"

"The newest one and the cheapest."

She took a sip of the tea and realized it wasn't as hot as she'd thought it was. "Perfect," she told Yancey with a smile.

"Well, I know you like it and since you're one of our favorite customers, we aim to please." He grinned at her. "So, any news?"

She thought for a moment and figured what the hell. "Yeah, I've got a date."

Yancey looked startled. "Oh? With Mark? Or Thad?"

She laughed. "Neither. I'm going out with an artist. Who didn't blink when I read his aura *and*," she said, leaning closer, "who's an empath."

"Really?" His gaze ran over her. "And when is this date?"

"Tonight." She couldn't help smiling.

He tilted his head to the side. "Very nice."

She took another drink of her tea as she watched Jay's fingers flying over the keyboard. She wondered if he was gifted in other ways. Maybe he just wasn't good with people, or with normal everyday things, but was a whiz on the PC. There were stranger things.

Then again, she'd seen the way Yancey was very protective of his brother, so that probably wasn't it.

Yancey muttered something about the back room. She finished off the tea as Jay finalized her order. "Should be here in three days."

Alyssa nodded and the room suddenly spun. Damn. Probably should have eaten today.

"That's..." She shook her head a little, hoping to clear it, but still things spun. "That's fine."

Get out! Get out! Run!

Her gaze rose to meet Jay's. She tried to focus on him but it was like looking down a long tunnel to his yellow eyes. Glowing. Were they glowing? The walls moved, waved.

She swallowed. Her mouth felt funny and thick, like when she went to the dentist and had to get a tooth pulled.

What the hell? The room tilted.

She took two steps and her legs gave out.

Oh shit.

She tried to reach for her phone clipped to her waist, her fingers fumbly.

The tea...

"Dad," she whispered, her gaze locked on the door. *Have to get out. Have to get out!*

The walls spun.

Something was pushing in on her. Threatening. Pushing, shoving, wanting in...

Fear roared up in her and she hurtled back to the car accident. Rolling, shattered glass, pain.

Her shields trembled. Lowered. Burst so quickly, pain iced through her head.

Pain, anger, *rage* slapped her and she screamed, but it only came out in the whisper of a moan.

Evil, dark and swirling, hissed out at her, sliced into her.

She turned and saw him.

The monster. Black fog. Red daggers, tendrils with wicked,

spiked arrows on the ends.

"No," she whispered.

"It's time," he hissed, his red eyes glowing...

Everything went black.

Chapter Thirteen

He looked at her lying on the floor, her hand near her phone. She'd tried. They always tried to get away. Why was that?

It would be so easy right now to take what he wanted.

But that wasn't how it was supposed to be. No, he had to wait. Just a little longer. He wanted the drug to wear off and that would take a while. Had she called her father? Had she managed to let him know where she was?

He looked at his brother. "You know we had to do this." His brother didn't say anything. He reached down and picked her up. "Close and lock the shop."

Her aura pulsed, slowly, blurring to the point where his own vision blurred and pain thrummed through his head.

He sensed her puny effort to keep him out. Yet the power surge to shatter her shields had still cost him. But shatter them he had, with such a force, he'd grabbed onto the counter to keep from going to his knees. She'd even moaned. He knew the moment she'd felt him. Felt him as if he were part of her, pushing against her, having her. He loved that moment, that first crack in their resistance. If it had been a few years ago, he would have enjoyed playing with her, taking her bit by bit until she conceded her power to him.

Taking it by force was fun too. And so damned heady it had

addicted him faster than even the meds he had to consume.

Pain stabbed through his skull, but he tried to ignore it. He had to ignore it. There were things to do. Things to ready.

Her to ready.

Time.

Time.

Time.

He could feel it slipping further and further away from him.

Her scent, young, innocent, yet worldly, rushed up his nostrils, calling to him, taunting him, *warning* him.

It would be so nice to take his time with her.

But time was something he just didn't have.

So he'd get her ready.

Ready for him.

For the transfer she'd give him. He shuddered at the feel of her power brushing alongside his. Fear, her fear trembled in her mind, wishing, needing to get away.

Aphrodisiac to him.

"Lake," she whispered.

He paused as he carried her to the hallway and the closet. He took a deep breath, already tired.

Lake. There was a thought.

Maybe he'd take them both.

Both... Excitement licked through his veins, hot and too tempting. Both. The transfers would be phenomenal.

Moving towards the closet, he shifted her so that he could open the door. She didn't weigh much, but then she'd just been getting her life back on track. If she was healthier, she'd be curvier.

He sighed, leaned over and nuzzled the side of her neck.

Innocence and power. Very heady. Very fragrant. Very alluring.

He wanted her.

He'd always wanted her. The way she moved called to him, hesitant, cautious, yet with purpose. Her power called to him, teasing, taunting, just waiting for him to claim what should be his.

Her power was his.

It really was a shame to see it end, to see her end.

Yet at the same time, anticipation coursed through him. He really couldn't wait.

This would be wonderful.

Setting her on the floor of the deep walk-in closet, he pressed a button on the side of the back wall, hidden just beside the rod. A back panel swung open to reveal his very special, very private room. He glanced over his shoulder, his brother would not bother him. His brother never bothered him. He'd always understood.

He smiled and bent to pick her up. This time, the walls tilted and he stumbled, knocking into the row of shelves lining one wall.

His brother appeared in the doorway. "You need help. You should go back to the doctor."

"Doctors said there was nothing they could do. This will help. She will help."

For a moment they stared at each other.

"I'll help you." His brother bent and picked her up, then carried her through the open doorway.

His brother was another reason he had to do this. The transfers had to work. He couldn't leave his brother.

Feeling weak, sick to his stomach, he followed.

He'd bought the building next to them several years ago

173

and had put in a connecting doorway that no one knew about. He'd also walled off two of the rooms. There were no windows. It was his special room.

His room to do with as he pleased, with whom he pleased.

And he had.

He had kept several others here before. Granted it wasn't as nice as the special place he'd had in California, but that was okay too. This one served its purpose. The simplicity of it was just what he needed. The walls were white so as to not draw attention from the power. Very important not to distract the power. White was the best. It kept the powers contained, kept them as they should be without distorting anything. The bed was white, the sheets white. Everything was white. He rather liked it that way. There was even a white stereo because he liked music as well. In the past he'd recorded them so he could play it back, hear the soft, begging sounds they made just before they died. He could almost relive it all in those moments.

He sighed and sat down in the white armchair. He watched as his brother laid her on the bed, excitement thrumming through him.

"Lake," she muttered yet again.

Lake. There was an idea...

He needed both of them.

The more he thought about it, the more he liked that idea.

He'd take both their transfers.

He'd never done two at once before. A *ménage* of sorts. He smiled, a plan forming in his mind. He looked down at her knowing he didn't have to bind her, she was too drugged.

Time, this gave him time to get things ready.

Lake...

❦

Lake pulled her shirt over her head and laughed as Max kissed her yet again.

"Alyssa will be home any minute," he said. "But she has a date tonight so I can always come over."

She smiled. "Maybe so." She kissed him back. "I'll have to think about it."

She bent down and pulled on her shoes. At least her clothing was in the studio, neatly folded, and she hadn't had to go searching for the articles. Been there, done that. Of course, their day had not started out as a foray into sex. Then again, she'd agreed to pose nude for a man she'd almost had on her couch, so it was probably a given. She'd never look at that beautiful chaise the same way again. Or gold gossamer for that matter.

She looked around the studio, the canvas he'd been painting of her, neatly covered with a cloth—damn it. She wanted to see it. She glanced to the corner where Alyssa's artwork stood leaning against the wall. One of Alyssa's paintings, the dark colors and twisted images all but screamed off the canvas. Alyssa...

"You think she'll be okay with us?"

He jerked on a blue Henley he'd grabbed from somewhere, his jeans still undone. God he was gorgeous.

"I don't see why not. Alyssa is Alyssa and if she'd had a problem with you, she would have said something. She's not shy about that, you know. I've a feeling she would have said something to you while you two meditated or whatever it is you do."

Again she smiled, then realized he was still worried about

the two of them. "You know, that is pretty much what we do. I'm trying to teach her to control her gift through practice and a healthy lifestyle."

"Control it?"

"Instead of it controlling her." She shrugged. "I've just been where she is. Well, not exactly, but I've been in the situation where I didn't understand what was happening to me, and the people I should have been able to count on to help me only made my life hell because I was different. There's nothing worse than not being able to be who you are. It really screws things up inside, ya know?"

"Yeah, I know and can't quite forgive myself for that one. Leaving her like I did."

She tilted her head and looked at him. "Alyssa will be fine. She's very powerful. But with her power comes a cost, from what I've learned. Either she learns to control her gift or it controls her. And you don't want the latter."

"I don't?"

She sighed and realized she wanted to go home, think and get dressed up for him. Then her mind switched back from what she'd wear to what they were talking about. "Some think that schizophrenic patients have psychic capabilities."

He nodded. "Some also believe they are the modern-day demon possessions."

"Either way, I don't want to see her go down that path when all she has to do is train herself to control her gift. So, yeah, I'll work with her. Reminding her to enjoy life, get out and do, to eat right, stay healthy, get plenty of rest. With meditation and concentration, she should learn how to maintain her shields so that she only reads, knows, sees what she wants."

He frowned. "What do you mean?"

"Well, with as powerful as she is, I wouldn't be surprised if she weren't an indigo."

Both brows rose. "Indigo?"

She waved a hand. "It's a term, slang for super psychic."

"Uh-huh."

At the skeptical note in his voice, she gave him her attention. "Well, take me. I can read auras. I pick up on emotions because of the auras and on rare, rare occasions, with those who I'm close to, I get an inkling when things aren't right or something might happen. The latter only twice in my life, so I don't think it really counts."

He shifted and buttoned his fly.

"So what's your specialty?" she asked him.

"Huh?"

"Well, your daughter got her gift from somewhere, and from what I've heard about your ex, it wasn't her."

For a moment he just stared at her. Then he sighed. "Mostly I just know when things are right. Sometimes, though it's been years, I knew when things were wrong."

"Wrong?"

"It happened more when I was younger than it has now that I'm older. Though with art, it's still there. I just follow my gut instinct on what will work and what won't. So far it's steered me right. I haven't gone bankrupt yet."

"Intuition. Got it."

"So, indigo?"

She pulled on her coat. "Well, Alyssa has them all, or at least a multitude of gifts." How to simplify? "Think super psychic for a very loose term. From her aura, I could see so much. She's intuitive, like you, but I think she's clairvoyant, more than likely her precognition is highly developed. Probably an empath, and from things she's mentioned to me, I wouldn't be surprised if she wasn't also a medium. The really strong ones usually are."

For a minute he didn't say anything.

She pulled her hair from under her collar and looked at him. "What?"

A frown wrinkled his brow as he stared at her.

"What?" she asked again, wondering what the hell she'd said to have put that look on his face.

"I knew she was special." He softly asked her, "You really think she's that gifted?"

"Yes," she answered without hesitating.

He sat on the edge of the chaise. "She's that gifted."

What was this? She studied him and wondered if he was okay. Maybe she should have explained it differently? She leaned over and kissed him on the cheek. "I'll leave you to your thoughts. I need to go home and change, especially if we're going out to eat." He was staring at the floor, his hands hanging between his knees.

Okay, so he definitely needed to think.

Without another word, she walked to the door.

"Lake?"

She turned, her hand on the knob.

His eyes were shuttered, his expression guarded, but still she felt the hurt and confusion waving off him, saw the regret shimmering in his aura.

"She always said, and I believed her..." He trailed off. "But her mother..." He shook his head. "And all this time, she's been to doctors, been medicated, told that she wasn't what she was." His eyes were filled with pain. "What kind of parent does that to their child?"

"Lots," she said with brutal honesty. "But in your case,

178

you've helped her. You know what she is, or you sensed it. You never tried to change her, and that is why she's thriving here."

He cocked a brow.

"She is. Even you said she's laughing, smiling. Some part of her has always known what she is, that she's different, and through it all, she's held on to that. That's amazing in and of itself. This is the first time in her life she's been able to accept who she is without fear, to explore and know she'll still be loved, still have a safe haven unconditionally."

He stared at her for a long moment, his expression more hopeful.

"Believe it. I do, and more importantly, Alyssa does."

She opened the door and he stood up. "Twenty minutes?"

She scoffed. "Darling, I may be beautiful, but dammit, I do have to work at it. Make it half an hour."

Like she could get in a shower and be ready that quickly. Actually, if she didn't wash her hair, she could do it. She'd wear the jeans with the black turtleneck. Amethyst pendant and earrings too.

Her boot heels clicked as she hurried down the steps and into the night. Damn, but it was cold. She took a deep breath. Snow was in the air. Probably snowing up in the mountains.

Coffee, she needed some coffee. She hurried across the street then stepped into the coffee shop, which was bustling tonight. Glancing around, she half expected to see Alyssa. She wasn't here, but Mark stood talking to a guy at the bar.

She checked her watch and saw that half an hour had passed since Alyssa's voice had floated through the loft warning them that she'd be home in—what had it been? Ten? No—fifteen minutes. Well, maybe she'd been gone longer than she'd thought.

No…

Fear crept in. Fear of what, exactly? That she should fear *for* or *of* something? Someone?

She tried to read what she was feeling but all she could sense was Alyssa.

"Mark?" she said, standing to the side of a young man wearing glasses.

"Hey, Lake." Mark shot the guy a tight smile. "What can I get for you?"

"Coffee. Whatever's on tap, as long as it's not decaf. There is just not a single reason for decaf."

He chuckled. "I know your opinion on the merits of caffeine."

The guy beside her turned. "I have to agree with you. And decaf espresso? I mean, who the hell came up with that?"

She smiled and looked back at Mark. "Have you seen Alyssa?"

The man beside her tensed. Blinking, she turned to him and stared, read him. His aura pulsed. Anxious, hopeful, and something else…

"Alyssa? From across the street?" he asked.

She only raised a brow.

"I'm Jonathan Murbanks."

The photos. She'd seen them in the studio, different ones in black frames, some noted to have no frames, just stretched over canvas. "Artist."

He smiled. "If you wait here for about twenty minutes, Alyssa will probably be here."

Now she gave him her full attention. Ah, the date. She vaguely wondered what Max would say when he found out about this. Was this considered mixing business with pleasure?

Then it hit her. The girl had wanted to get ready for her date, and knowing Alyssa, she wouldn't have been late. Lake checked her cell phone to see if there were any messages, but there weren't. Not a single one.

Huh.

Maybe Alyssa didn't need girl advice. Just as well, what would she give her after all? And the advice she *could* give her, she wouldn't. Max would not approve. Then again, every girl needed a safe-sex speech, but she figured with Alyssa, the girl had already had that one.

So where was she?

Upstairs? She studied Murbanks again and realized he was trying to read her as well. Shielding did have its uses.

She shut the eager young man out and tried to focus on Alyssa but got nothing.

Don't panic. No need to panic.

But her hands were shaking.

"What's wrong?" Murbanks asked.

She just looked at him, trying to get a read on Alyssa, but...

"You're scared," he stated.

"Mark, where's Alyssa?"

Mark looked from one to the other and finally said, "I don't know. I saw her earlier, but I haven't seen her in a while." He looked down the street. "She pissed Thad off and headed down that way."

"Did she say where she was going?"

He shook his head. "No, what's wrong?"

She started to tell him she was worried about Alyssa but decided against it. "Nothing, I'm sure. Maybe she's upstairs waiting for me."

Mark's expression didn't change as he stared at her. "Why?"

Deciding not to worry them all or start a panic attack, she said, "I'm sure it's nothing. I just thought we were getting ready together. For our dates," she added with a glance at the artist. "But I guess I misunderstood."

"Did you check her house?" Mark asked.

She nodded. "I just came from there. I'll head upstairs and see what the deal is."

Fear rippled along her spine as she hurried through the shop to the back door. There she took the stairs two at a time up to her apartment. Pulling the key from her pocket, she shoved it home.

Her phone rang and she paused to answer it. Maybe it was Alyssa.

"Hello?"

"Hi," Max's voice floated over the phone. "Listen, I was just curious, will it really take you half an hour to get ready? You look fine the way you are." There was something in his voice.

"Why?"

For a moment he said nothing, then, "I don't know. Just a weird feeling I have in the pit of my stomach."

Shit. "Have you seen Alyssa?"

Again the silence. "No, I was wondering where she was. Maybe she met up with her date early?"

"No. I just met him downstairs in the coffee shop. She's not there. Mark hasn't seen her either."

Fear was a sly beast, shifting this way and that so she couldn't tell if she could read her feelings correctly or not.

"Maybe she'll show up in the next few minutes." He took a deep breath. "Why don't you come back over here and wait for her with me, then when we both see she's okay, we'll go eat."

He was worried too.

She stepped through the door, her apartment dark except from the streetlights.

"Let me just change my shirt and then I'll be right back over there."

"No." Then he huffed. "Sorry, sorry. Okay, but hurry, something's off."

She couldn't agree more. "I'll be there in less than five minutes."

Lake hung up and reached in to turn on the light.

Darkness slithered through the air, a second's warning before evil struck.

She ducked but she wasn't quite quick enough. Pain exploded in her skull, radiating down her body. Spots danced before her eyes and the world tilted, the floor rushing up to meet her. Blood roared in her ears, but still she heard him. "No you won't."

Keep moving. Keep moving. Have to keep moving.

"Now where do you think you're going? You have to come with me, Lake. I have something, or rather someone, who might interest you," he said softly.

Who the hell was he? He was vaguely familiar but she couldn't place him, couldn't...

Max...

"I wanted to take you back to share the whole process with her," the voice hissed, closer.

She tried to get to her feet, but the room still spun and twirled. Bile rose up hot and thick in the back of her throat. Slipping, she fell back again, hoping she wouldn't be sick.

Move! Move! Move!

His steps weren't hurried. Instead, he just stood there staring at her.

Short. He's too damned short. Rather round, but the power behind the blow he'd dealt her was very, very strong. His stature was not given to fat, it was all solid muscle.

The edges of her vision blurred and she blinked. She touched the back of her neck, not surprised to feel the stickiness of blood.

"You're very powerful, did you know that?" he whispered.

His whisper reminded her of slithering snakes, hissing, whispering, quiet and threatening.

"Wh-why are you here?"

He just looked at her and she saw his face morph into two, then three before slowly melding back to one.

"Because I need you. Alyssa might not be enough." He walked closer, standing over her.

Alyssa? What the hell did this rat bastard know about Alyssa. "Wh-where is she?" She blinked and tried to get up, slipping.

He tsked. "You'll only hurt yourself."

She looked up at him. His eyes were a strange color. Yellow-green hazel, but not in a pleasant way. They were cold eyes. Eyes that saw too much.

Lake tried to take a deep breath, tried to focus and steady herself. His scent engulfed her. Incense and...medicine. She studied him but couldn't read or see his aura.

No aura?

Chills danced over her spine. *Alyssa... Oh my God.* His words uttered just moments before terrified her. *"Alyssa might not be enough."*

He had no aura.

No aura? No aura. No soul.

She focused harder, felt the air shift, the ice of evil, the darkness that waited just there at the edges. The same evil she'd sensed several nights ago on the street when she'd run into Alyssa. Evil. Black aura. No soul.

Her breath froze in her lungs and she tried again to focus on him, but it was of little use. *Have to get up. Move. Move. Move.*

"Wh-what do you want?"

No use. Her head swam and all she could see were those eyes.

Eyes that sucked her in.

Deeper... Deeper...

"I've already said. I want you. What you can give me."

"What is that?" she asked.

He leaned down closer and she sensed decay, just as the snakes hissed at the edge of her perception.

"Your power," he whispered, his breath hot and pungent.

Max paced the studio.

Something was wrong. He could *feel* it. Anxiety skittered over his nerves. He hadn't been completely honest with Lake. Not that he had intended to lie to her, but he'd never told anyone about his...*knowing.* He'd mentioned it to her, yes. His grandmother had known of his ability to sense things. He'd always just called it instinct. His ex-wife had known and yet hadn't. Things beyond what she could actually see and feel had frightened her.

Thus the end of their marriage in more ways than one. She'd called him a freak and he hadn't defended himself. Hadn't stayed around to defend his kids. The daughter who almost died and the son who had. Had Timothy been gifted as well? Would he have even mentioned it if he was? Or was he like his father and hid his abilities for fear of ridicule? At least Alyssa had never done that. Never once had she really tried to hide who she was. Granted, she'd shoved herself aside to try to fit into the mold her mother had thought was right and proper, but it hadn't worked.

Max rubbed a hand over his face. Hell, his daughter had the scars on her wrists to prove it hadn't worked. Her attempted suicide several years earlier had warned him but the court had ruled in favor of his ex. What court wouldn't? She had to be the sane one. Her grandmother hadn't claimed to be a witch. Her family hadn't had several members claim to have special abilities.

The court shrinks had ripped his family apart and he'd stood back and let them, his own head filling with self-doubt.

But now?

He paced and worried, glancing at the clock as fear wrapped tight bands around his chest.

How long did it take to change a shirt and get over here? Lake had known something was up. He could tell the way her voice held no emotion, as if she was trying to shield him from something. From what?

He pressed the message again, Alyssa's voice filling the air.

"Dad, it's me, I just wanted you to know I'm going to be home in about fifteen minutes after I get the Grimm Brothers to order this book I want." She took a deep breath, pausing before continuing, *"I've got to get ready."* He heard the smile in her voice. *"I've got a date."*

A date...

With whom? She might be nineteen, but he needed to know she was all right. That she was okay because he had the distinct impression that she was anything but.

Hell.

It was like the time before. Before when he'd ignored it and then the call had come. The call telling him that his daughter was in the hospital from a car accident.

If he'd paid attention, would things be different?

Did it even matter? Probably not. What was important was the here and now. Right now what he needed was...

Fear and darkness slammed into him.

He staggered and grabbed the door frame of the hallway. What the hell was that?

Panic skittered over his skin.

Lake?

Alyssa?

Dad...

Max...

Lake.

He shook his head, the strange feeling slowly slipping away. He picked up the phone and dialed Lake's number. Expecting her to answer, anger flared through him when her voice mail picked up.

Maybe it was just the connection.

He hit redial, but again it went to voice mail.

What had she said? She'd be right over here. Okay, so it hadn't been exactly five minutes yet. He was starting to act like a jealous idiot, but he couldn't help it.

He paced for several more minutes. To hell with this.

Grabbing his jacket, he paused at the door where the white board hung. He scrawled a note to Alyssa: *CALL me ASAP~Dad.*

Hurrying from the loft, he pulled on his jacket and ran across the street, barely missing an oncoming car and almost taking out a pair of lovers wrapped up in each other near the entrance of the coffee shop.

"Damned tourists," he muttered.

He strode into the coffee shop. Mark and Jonathan sat at the bar, looking up as he neared.

"What's wrong?" Mark asked.

He glanced from one to the other. "Have either of you seen Alyssa?"

"Is something wrong with her?" Jonathan asked.

Max only shook his head and focused on Mark.

"I just told Lake not ten minutes ago that she was here and then she left."

The panic gripped inside, strangling him.

"We're sorry to inform you that your son did not survive the crash that also claimed your ex-wife... Your daughter is in critical condition in our surgical intensive care unit... touch and go through the night..."

From before or now? What the hell was happening? He didn't have a clue, but he knew he had to find out—and he had to find out fast.

"Lake still upstairs?"

Mark jerked his head to the back. "Yes."

He turned to go and then said over his shoulder, "If Alyssa comes in, keep her here."

"Why?"

"Just do it." He wasn't going to explain.

He hurried out into the cold bite of wind.

Something crashed upstairs and he cursed, all but flying up the stairs. "Lake!"

The door was locked.

He pounded on it

"Ma—" Lake's scream cut off.

He rammed his shoulder against the door, but the damned thing held.

"Lake! Lake!"

This time, the wood shifted, giving beneath him. Cursing, Max pulled back and kicked the edge near the handle. The door swung inward.

For a moment he didn't see her, didn't see them. A crash in the kitchen had him whirling in that direction. Lake stood weaving, holding a pan. A man lay moaning at her feet.

"Bastard!" She lifted the pan to hit him again, and Max dashed forward to grab her arm. She tried to jerk it away.

Blood at the base of her neck caught his attention.

"Are you hurt?" he asked.

She jerked her arm away, but he wrestled the pan away from her. She was hurt. Damn it. Rage hazed his vision.

She swayed and he caught her. He glanced down at a man he'd known for years. Mr. Yancey Narton.

"What?"

"Get the hell away from me. Bastard," she muttered.

He assumed she was talking about the man on the ground. "You've all but bashed his skull in with Calphalon. I think he's down."

She looked at him with glazed eyes and said, "Alyssa... He knows..."

She passed out in his arms.

Cursing, he looked at her attacker, then back at her. His rage roared into fury. Yancey stared up at the ceiling not blinking. From here Max could see he was still breathing. Carefully, he laid Lake on the floor and grabbed the cordless phone on the floor beside Yancey.

"Where's my daughter?"

He dialed nine-one-one.

The son of a bitch only stared at the ceiling.

Chapter Fourteen

Where was she?

No one knew where Alyssa was. He paced the police station. Noises filtered through, voices in the background, ringing phone, someone cursing as something dropped. Max ignored it all.

Lake had been taken to the emergency room, even though she didn't think she needed to go. Not go? He hadn't taken no for an answer, and thankfully neither had the EMS personnel. Hard-headed woman—thank God. If her skull hadn't been as thick as it was, she might have a hell of a lot worse than a concussion.

He'd since learned that the man they all knew as Yancey Narton, owner of The Book Emporium & More, was an alias. He was wanted in three states as a person of interest in the disappearance and murder of several young women and men.

"Did your daughter ever mention Mr. Narton bothering her?" someone asked. There were three detectives and the chief of police in the station, along with county sheriff personnel. He vaguely remembered someone saying how the state boys would probably be coming in and an argument about the FBI.

Max didn't give a shit who all was involved. He just wanted his daughter found. He should have paid closer attention, known what all was going on, who she spent her time with. But he'd wanted to give her space. He hadn't wanted to seem like he was smothering, or being too controlling. She'd had enough of that in her life. More than enough. He'd wanted to give her freedom.

And that decision might just have gotten her...

He shuddered and raked his hands over his face.

"Mr. Gray?"

He paused and looked at the balding, short man who'd asked the question. "What?"

"Did your daughter—"

"Her name is Alyssa," he snapped.

The balding detective raised one brow, but nodded. "Alyssa." He cleared his throat. "Did Alyssa ever mention a problem with Mr. Narton?"

He tried to think. Finally, he shook his head. "No, she mentioned one of the Howard boys not getting the picture. The older one, I think. Thad, the charmer." Had she mentioned the bookstore owner? And what if they were wrong? What if her disappearance had nothing to do with the damned bookstore? Where was she? "Have you asked Yancey or Narton or whoever the fuck he is?"

It seemed like everyone took a collective breath. "He's in a coma."

Max couldn't have heard them correctly. He blinked.

"Could she have taken off without telling anyone?" someone else asked. Max had no idea who and he didn't care. He didn't want to be here answering these questions. What he wanted were answers.

"Why aren't you out there looking for my daughter? Why are you here? Just sitting here asking questions? Why aren't you *doing* something?" He didn't want to wait around, he *needed* answers. He wanted to know where Alyssa was and, damn it, he wanted her home. Home where she was supposed to be. Home where she was safe. Home where he didn't have to worry about her.

"Mr. Gray, we realize this is a difficult time for you and—"

"Someone should be out there looking for my daughter not in here fucking around."

Another man pushed away from the wall and walked up to Max. He'd been introduced but Max didn't remember the guy's name or rank or even who the hell he was with. Nor did he care.

"Mr. Gray, this may all seem pointless but the more we know, the better our chances of finding your daughter." Hard, cold brown eyes stared at him. They were the same height, but this guy was bigger, harder somehow than the others here. "You are our only link to her. We need your help to better understand her. Once we understand her, know her habits, we'll know her and the chances of finding her increase." Those eyes didn't look away from him. "Normally, we wouldn't even be talking to you until tomorrow, but I'm going to be straight with you."

Something bad. It was something bad. He knew it with every fiber of his being.

"We found a victim..."

Max didn't hear anything else, his world stopped, his blood froze and he couldn't breathe.

Someone helped him to a chair but he shrugged them off.

"I'm sorry, what?" he asked, focusing back on the man who'd been speaking to him.

"The young female was reported missing a couple of days ago. We believe the perpetrator of this crime is someone we've been searching for, for some time. The only link we have is that the victim had called a friend to say she was going to a

193

bookshop." The man sat in the chair beside him and said, "In light of this evening's events, that your daughter was last known going to that bookshop is of utmost interest to us. We are looking for Alyssa and will continue to do everything in our power to find her." Those hard eyes gave no mercy. "But we need you to help us do that. You being upset is understandable, being frustrated is as well. However, if you can't help us, then you hinder us and that we won't allow."

Max finally shook his head and said, "I get it. That makes sense." He fisted his hands, then flexed them. Fist. Flex. He had to do *something*.

"What do you need to know?"

The man gave him a small smile. "Everything."

Lake stared at the ceiling. Someone or something hammered spikes into her skull. God, her head...

She wished Max was here, but knew he was needed elsewhere.

Alyssa...

She shivered as she remembered the way the man had been in her apartment, the way he'd been...so calm, she realized. He'd been so calm, as if attacking her for her power, whatever the hell that was, was the most normal thing in the world.

Those strange golden eyes, cold as a shark's, lit with some inner fire.

"You doing okay?" a nurse asked. What was her name? Betty? Beatrice? Bethany. She was just too damned perky. The woman's aura was bright yellow, like a sunflower or a bouncing butterfly.

Made her head hurt even worse. "When can I have some pain meds?"

The nurse just smiled. "I know it hurts, but just a little longer. Then the doc will be here."

Bethany did something with the charts and Lake tried to calm herself. She should probably call Cora, but if she did that, Cora would freak and be on the first plane here. Along with Rogan, who would get all protective and annoying. Friends were great, but she just didn't want them here and her friends would make things...difficult.

The lights hurt her eyes, so she put her arm carefully across her face, to shield the harsh lights.

"What happened to the man?" she asked Bethany, without opening her eyes. "The other person they brought in...the man who attacked me. Is he here?"

"That coma guy?"

She opened her eyes and tried to sit up, pain slashing through her skull. Gasping back a moan and cursing her own weakness she asked, "Coma? No, he was brought in with me."

"Yeah, well, the guy's got a brain tumor the size of..." Bethany shook her head. "Don't you worry about him, honey. He's not going to be bothering anyone ever again."

But Alyssa. Where was she? Did he know? Had he said? She tried to think, to feel, but nothing came. Oh, God.

She licked her dry lips and said, "Did he say anything? When they brought him in? Did he say *anything?*"

She looked from Bethany to the wide picture window that gave a lovely view of the active ER desk beyond. From here she could see the black uniform of a police officer standing outside a door. Was that his room? Who the hell was the guy?

Bethany tilted her head and checked something else. "Honey, he didn't say anything, already slipped into the coma when they brought him in. Cops are still guarding him, but he's in a coma. He's not saying anything."

Bouncy people could be very talkative. Lake figured Ms. Bethany was probably not supposed to tell her that. Then again, this was probably the highlight of the evening, possibly the week.

Bethany leaned closer over the bed, looking behind her. "Are you feeling better?" she asked softly. "The cops want to talk to you as soon as possible."

She wished she had some serious pain meds. "Why?"

"Something 'bout a missing girl."

Missing girl—Alyssa.

"I'll talk to them. Though please tell them I'd like someone who knows what is going on, and not to be pawned off on a rookie. I can't decide if I'm going to throw up or just die from my headache. Neither sounds good and I don't want to go through it twenty thousand times." Though she figured she'd have to anyway, whether she wanted to or not.

Jay looked down at the girl, still and prone on the bed. So pretty. She was always so pretty. He liked her. He'd always liked her.

He rubbed his hands over his arms. Where was Yancey? Yancey should have been back by now, shouldn't he? What if he was sick somewhere? What would he do?

What should he do? Did he go get him and leave the girl here?

Yancey had told him to stay here, to watch her. So he had. Pretty Alyssa. Strange Alyssa. Yancey had said powerful Alyssa. Did she have power? Power to cure his brother?

Jay sat down, pulling his knees to his chest, and waited. He waited and he watched. He watched her. She was really pretty and she was always so nice to him. So sweet. She never treated him like he was stupid. Not like the others, not like some who came into the shop and looked at him as if he didn't know what he was doing. She'd always asked him how he was, if he was feeling fine. If he could help her.

And he always wanted to help her.

He wanted to help her now.

But his brother...

Yancey needed help. Yancey needed her power.

What did he do?

Jay patted his legs.

Pat.

Pat.

Pat.

What was he supposed to do? What would Yancey want him to do?

"Just stay here and watch her."

So he was, watching her sleep. Why he had to watch her sleep, he wasn't exactly certain, but that's what Yancey wanted.

Her face was pale, paler than normal. So white in the white room that her hair reminded him of a dark blob. The dark blobs on white the doctors made him look at. Still and perfect just like a doll.

It wouldn't stay that way...

He shook his head. No. No. No.

He knew what she would look like after Yancey had gotten through with her. She'd have dark marks on that long neck. Beautiful neck. So small, so easy to squeeze. He knew that. Yancey had let him play before. Play with Yancey.

He shut his eyes and shook his head. No. No. No. He wouldn't do that to her. Not to Alyssa. Pretty Alyssa.

Where was Yancey?

He listened carefully, and could hear them. Just beyond the wall. The wall with the secret panel. Footsteps beat hard against the floor. Voices carried. Some orders barked. Other words were garbled and made no sense.

But he also heard them calling her name.

He could turn on the music, but he knew that the music could be heard from this room. He'd heard it before, but then he knew to listen for it. He knew what his brother did when the music played.

"Alyssa!"

"Miss Gray!"

"Can you hear us?"

"Are you hurt?"

She wasn't hurt. He didn't hurt them. His brother didn't really hurt them. They were set free. Free... No longer bound by the power.

"Police!"

Carefully, so as to not make a sound on the hard floor, he crawled over to her and sat beside her bed.

The lights shone down on her dark, spiky hair, shiny...soft. How soft? Like silk? Or like the bunny he used to have before he'd let it go.

Let it go.

Let her go.

Keep her.

Watch her.

Had to watch her. He reached out, but pulled his hand back before he touched her.

Soft...

"Pretty Alyssa," he whispered. Blood pounded against his ears, his heart thundered, and he simply wanted to touch her.

Couldn't wake her up. Shouldn't wake her up. She'd be upset then and that would never be good. Didn't want to wake her, wake her, wake her.

Touch her.

Touch her.

Jay reached out, paused and finally touched her hair. Softer, and thicker than he thought.

He'd never understood why Yancey did what he did. He didn't ask his brother, not really. Yancey was his brother. He'd always been his brother. Yancey always helped him, took up for him when others were being mean. But he'd always felt sorry for the girls.

Pretty.

She was so pretty. He leaned down and breathed deep, inhaled a scent that filled his senses and made him take another breath. He shuddered. Sweet and innocent, reminding him of honeysuckle.

Memories slammed into him, jerking him back.

He remembered the first girl, years ago. That scent. *No. No. No.*

A heavy southern evening, bathed in late golden light. Honeysuckle vines all around them as his brother squeezed the life out of the young blonde girl. The bees had buzzed, dancing with the late evening dragonflies. So long ago, yet it seemed like only yesterday.

She'd been soft too. He couldn't remember her name, but he could see her. And he remembered the honeysuckle.

Blinking, he finally came back to the white room. The room where Alyssa lay, unbound on the bed. Jay shook his head, trying to clear the images from it.

He knew the power that coursed through him when his brother killed someone. His brother had been known to let him play. The power was a rush like he'd never known, but he also knew the sickness that ate him.

What to do? What to do? What to do?

He wished he knew. Wished he could figure it out.

Yancey would kill her. Yancey would take her, wrapping his hands around her neck until she begged, her eyes...

He always remembered their eyes. There was something very strong about the eyes. Eyes were windows to the soul. And if the soul died, he knew you could see it in the eyes. They went flat, opaque. No life. No soul. No power.

His brother needed power, needed it to heal, to get better.

If Yancey didn't get better, he could die. Jay knew that, his brother had told him. He knew that Yancey needed this. Needed her.

Jay ran his hand over her hair again, softly petting her. Taking another deep breath, he watched as he trailed his hand over her chest. Small breasts, small waist...

The blood pounded harder inside him.

Harder. Harder. Harder.

He wanted her. Wanted her so he could feel that bolt of power that shot through him like it had before when he'd helped his brother, watched his brother.

But should he?

No.

No.

Yes.

He glanced again at the door and knew that the police were still out there, searching, hoping to find her.

But they wouldn't find her until he was ready.

Until Yancey was ready. But that shouldn't be too much longer.

Where was his brother?

Yancey needed to hurry, needed to come so that Jay would know what to do. So that he'd know if he was supposed to fix this or not.

What if the police happened to find them? What was he supposed to do?

He touched her again, lower than he had before, just below the buttons on her low slung jeans.

"So pretty," he whispered leaning over her and pressing his lips to hers.

She shifted, moaned.

Jay stilled.

Where was Yancey?

The scent of her filled his nostrils and he had to taste her again. This time, he left his lips on hers, soft, firm, cool against his.

He closed his eyes and wondered if he could take her power for his brother? Then he could give it to Yancey.

He closed his mouth more firmly over hers and sighed. "Pretty Alyssa. I like you."

Lake answered more questions and more questions. She really wanted those pain meds now. Apparently she'd grappled with a deranged man.

Hell, she already knew that. She hardly needed the cops telling her this.

Where was Max? She had no clue, but she'd like to know. How was he? Probably not too good. He loved his daughter, he worried about her. He worried about her a lot. He'd be going out of his loving mind.

Lake should be there for him. She knew that without a shadow of a doubt.

"Did he say anything else, Ms. Johnson?" the policeman asked.

She took a deep breath and smelled the stringent scent of cleaning supplies overlaying the pungent scent of stale urine. Perfume de hospital.

Closing her eyes, she leaned back against the pillow and said again, "No. All he said was that he wanted my power and that I would help him or something. And he said, 'Alyssa might not be enough'."

"Enough what?"

How many times were they going to ask her the same questions over and over and over?

"Power, I think," she told him honestly this time.

"But what type of power?"

Sighing, she finally looked at him. "I know you ran me. I know what you think of me."

His eyes crinkled at the edges. "Oh, I doubt that, Ms. Johnson."

She only stared at him.

"Well, it's not every day we come across a..."

"Aura reader."

"Right."

"See?"

He shook his head and ran a hand over his face.

"Look, Detective."

"It's actually agent."

She didn't care. "Whatever. I see auras. I have for years and years and yours is..." She dropped her shields and focused. Pain shot through her head and she hissed.

He didn't say anything until she met his gaze again, this time her vision was slightly blurred.

"You were saying?" His salt and peppered brow arched.

"Damaged. Your aura is damaged. Slashed."

He jerked ever so slightly. Those eyes met hers square on. She held the stare and waited. Finally, he cleared his throat. "About Mr. Narton."

"I've told you all I know."

"What was his aura like?"

She thought back to those moments that she'd tried to read him. No aura...

"He didn't have one," she whispered.

"What?"

"He didn't have one. Blank, black. He had a black aura. Pure evil." She held his gaze again, expecting some sort of smart-ass reply or derogatory remark.

Instead, he only narrowed his gaze at her. "There is such a thing as real evil in this world."

She snorted. "Really? I had no idea. What with last year and the psycho who almost killed my best friend? The Angel

Eye killer?"

His lips compressed.

"Yes. I know. Evil is real. Some people use the term loosely, but it's there. Been here for eons. And it will always be." Why she said that, she didn't know, but there it was.

This time he flipped his little book shut. He'd stopped taking notes half an hour ago. At her bedside, he patted her hand. "Most never see it, never sense it, Ms. Johnson. You're very gifted."

"Thank you."

"I'll let you get some sleep."

Like that was going to happen. "Agent?"

He turned at the door and she saw and felt his weariness shimmering brown at the edge of his aura.

"Where is Max? Mr. Gray?"

He took a deep breath. "He's still at the station."

She nodded and studied the waffle weave of the thin white hospital blanket. He was there. She was here. And where the hell was Alyssa?

Commotion from outside her room drew her attention. A gurney was wheeled through another set of doors as medical personnel barked orders in acronyms and numbers that meant nothing to her.

To hell with this. It wasn't like she was getting any sleep anyway. She shoved the blanket away, moving slowly as she swung her legs to the side of the bed. Carefully, she pulled the IV from the back of her hand and pressed down as blood welled. Needles were so not her favorite thing.

At least she still had her clothing on. She'd been told that she'd get a gown when she was admitted upstairs to the hospital. As yet that hadn't happened. Thankfully. Okay, so her head hurt like someone had hit it with a sledgehammer, but it was like a migraine, right? A really bad, really painful, fucking migraine.

She could do this.

On the little table-rolling-cart thing beside her bed, she grabbed a band-aid and slapped it over the IV spot and huffed out a breath.

So she had a concussion, and her head hurt.

At the doorway, she noticed everyone seemed busy. Fine by her. She shuffled her way down the hallway to the exit.

"And where do you think you're going?" a voice asked from beside her.

She didn't have to turn to know it was the agent who had been asking her questions. Salt and peppered hair, trimmed ruthlessly short, and flat dark eyes that had undoubtedly seen too much. "Out of here."

The edges of his eyes creased again as he narrowed his gaze. "Don't like hospitals?"

"Not my favorite places. No."

"You should probably be back in bed."

She crossed her arms over her chest. "I'm going to the police station, where I assume Max is pacing back and forth snarling at everyone. If you don't like that, too bad. And if you help me, we can get out of here without anyone from the hospital finding me and making me read pages after pages of release forms until my headache worsens to the point I'll stay just so I won't have to read another word."

One corner of his mouth kicked up and she realized he was actually rather handsome when he smiled. Lines bracketed his mouth. He sighed, glanced back over his shoulder, gave a single nod to another plain-clothed man standing outside Mr. Narton's door with the other policeman.

Agents, huh? She wondered if they were with the state or the Feds. Did New Mexico even have an investigation bureau? Or a variation thereof? Then again, he probably was FBI. He looked like what she imagined a federal agent to look like. All business, no humor.

Which meant he'd be here only because Mr. Narton had been wanted for other crimes in other states. She shivered, remembering the way his hot breath had skimmed her cheek, the way his soulless eyes had been filled with an unholy fire.

She shivered again.

"You're not here with the state guys, are you?" She rubbed her arms as they stepped out into the night.

He didn't say anything.

"Are you?"

"No," he answered and led her to a Crown Vic.

She didn't say anything else as she slid into the car and waited for him to get into the driver's side.

When the heat blew from the heaters, she said, "There are more, aren't there?"

For a moment he didn't answer her. Then he took a deep breath. "We're investigating."

Which was an answer in and of itself without actually answering her.

"I bet you did good in Hedging Answers 101."

She leaned her forehead against the cool window and tried to ignore the pain slamming against her skull until they pulled up in front of the police station. Not waiting for the silent agent, she hurried into the station. She pulled the doors open, wincing at the bright light as she stepped into the warmth.

A phone rang on the front desk, ricocheting knives in her

head. A cuffed man in dirty clothes yelled obscenities at a cop standing next to him.

She looked past them, searching for...

"He's in the conference room," her hospital rescuer told her.

She followed him back behind the desk, along the wall and down a hallway. At the end was a large room and there sat Max.

He sat with his head in his hands, his shoulders slumped. A Styrofoam cup sat in front of him.

Her heart squeezed. Taking a deep breath, she walked into the room and pulled out the chair beside him. Max didn't look up. She put her hand on his wrist and he lifted his head. Surprise, shock, relief. The skin on his lean face was stretched taut, his cheekbones standing out.

He frowned. "What are you doing here?"

She only arched a brow.

"You're supposed to be in the hospital." His frown deepened. "You should be in the hospital. Why aren't you in the hospital? You have a damned concussion."

She laced her fingers with his. "I walked out."

He blinked, then blinked again. "You walked out, just like that?"

"Yep. Felt I was needed more here."

His sigh huffed warmly on her face. "You need another head scan."

She smiled. "Nah, hard as rocks, my head."

He scoffed and stared at the cup of coffee. Finally, he picked it up and took a sip, wincing.

"Cop coffee is always terrible."

"Spend a lot of time in police stations?"

She shrugged. "A bit. I just watch television and read. All

cop coffee, even fictional, is bad. Really bad. Like mud."

He propped his elbow on the table and rested his temple against his fisted hand. "They haven't found her yet, Lake." His eyes, those normally lively gray eyes, were filled with pain, turbulent with emotions she couldn't imagine let alone name.

"We'll find her."

A muscle bunched in his cheek. "We have to. I can't..." He bit down and shifted his gaze away from hers.

Lake squeezed his hand. "We will."

His gray eyes met hers again.

"We will."

His Adam's apple bobbed as he swallowed. "I knew, I knew something was wrong, but didn't act quickly enough. I knew."

"Your actions saved me, Max. If not for you, I'd be dead. And since I'm not, we have a clue where Alyssa might or might not be."

He frowned.

She scooted her chair closer. "You followed your instincts and I thank you for that."

"It's going to be dawn soon," he finally muttered, sliding the almost empty coffee cup back and forth on the table. "Where the hell is she? It's snowing in the mountains. Is she cold, is she..." He swallowed again. "What if—"

"Don't." She cupped his face. "Do *not* play the what-if game, you'll go freaking insane. We. Will. Find. Her."

She hoped to hell she was right and it wasn't too late. She didn't think it was because Narton had said he didn't know if Alyssa would be enough. Not that she *wasn't* enough. So in Lake's opinion, Alyssa was still alive. The question was where and why no one had heard from her since late the night before. Where had the man stashed her?

What-if's were dangerous. They could play the what-if game until the end of time.

A movement in the doorway had her turning in her seat.

"Agent?"

"Morrow. Sorry, never introduced myself." He stepped into the room. "Narton had a brother that we've heard about, known about, but we can't find him either."

Max tensed beside her. "You think he has her? Or that he's involved?"

Morrow didn't say anything for a minute. Then he took a deep breath. "Initially, no, we didn't, but at present, we're not ruling out the possibility that the brother could be or is involved."

"And?"

Morrow opened his mouth to say something, then thought better of it because he shut his mouth, thought for a moment before adding, "And, we're working on all the leads we have."

Which meant jack in her opinion.

"Have you searched the bookstore?" Max asked.

"Yes, Mr. Gray, the bookstore has been searched. We're also looking at the buildings beside them."

Max nodded once, then again. Standing, he pulled her to her feet. "I'm tired of sitting around here. We're going home. Lake will be with me."

The agent looked from one to the other. "You should stay at home in case someone calls."

Max glanced at his watch. "For the last ten hours no one has been at my house to answer a phone, other than cops. I figure we're good."

He walked out of the room, and since he had hold of her hand, she followed him out. The cold morning air sucked her breath from her lungs.

When they were in his car, he sat staring out the windshield.

"You want me to drive?"

He shook his head and started the car. "I can't just sit in there doing nothing any more, Lake. I have to get out and *do* something."

"I know. I'll help you. Where do you want to start?"

He drove, single mindedly. "The bookstore."

"Sounds like a plan."

Alyssa opened her eyes. Gritty as sandpaper. She reached up to rub them and realized she hurt. All over. Car accident? Another car accident. Mom?

No, Mom was dead.

God, her head. Someone with a gong and a ten-piece brass band was having a damned party in her skull.

She moaned and blinked. Where was she? White. All she saw was white. What the hell?

This time she blinked until everything focused. White walls, white counter, white floor. Glancing over, she saw there was even a white stereo. She was on white sheets.

Was she dead?

Then she rolled over and screamed.

Jay sat there, not two feet away, staring at her, his legs pulled up against his chest. His yellow eyes staring at her, just staring.

She shivered, chills dancing over her skin.

What had happened...?

Images, disjointed and scattered, flitted through her brain. *The coffee shop...Mark...a date with Jonathan... Have to get ready.*

The bookshop...Jay and his eyes...Yancey...her book.

She frowned, trying to remember.

Then?

Instead of images, emotions smoked to life. Fear, not just fear, terror slammed into her and her breath froze in her lungs. Desire, rage and...evil.

Evil...

That essence she'd experienced before, following her, stalking her, trapping her. It floated in this room, not dark and black. No, but like the scent of smoke lingering long after the fires have gone out, long after the smoke no longer swirled through the air, the scent would remain, noxious. Here it was the same. A thick layer of the remnants of evil slithered over her spine.

Neither of them moved. She lay on the bed, half rolled over. He sat still, in the same position, just staring at her.

Carefully, she moved, pulled her legs up and sat straight. "Wh—" She had to clear her throat and swallow past the cotton taste of her mouth. "What am I doing here?"

He narrowed his eyes as he stared at her. "You have to help us."

Us? She didn't glance around, but tried to feel another person. They were the only ones here.

"Do you mean your brother?"

He tilted his head to the side. "He's sick."

Really? Never would have guessed that one.

"Where am I?"

"Between."

She frowned. "Between what?"

His fingers started to fidget. "Between."

"Between..."

"The buildings. The worlds. The powers." He nodded. "The power."

Fear hissed up her backbone, but she ignored it. Fear was not going to help her here. *Think. Think. Think.*

Glancing around the room, she saw the door past him. The lighting caught the darker outline on the wall just right or she might not have seen it. Even the damned hinges and doorknob were white. What the hell was with the white anyway?

"Can't leave. Have to watch you," he whispered, jerking her attention back to him.

"But I need to leave, Jay," she said calmly.

He shook his head back and forth, back and forth, his fingers tapping against his legs. "Have to watch you."

"Why?"

"He told me to." Taptaptaptaptap.

His fingers were distracting. "Who told you to?"

"Brother. Have to listen. Have to do what he wants."

"Why?"

He blinked and frowned at her, his yellow eyes narrowing. "He's sick."

And they were back to that. "How sick is he?"

He picked at a spot on his jeans and dropped his eyes to what he was doing. "Told him to go to the doctor. Doctors can help him, but he says no. Hurt in his head, and he needs their power to heal him."

Power? "Whose power?"

He kept picking at the spot.

"Whose power, Jay?"

"The special ones. The gifted ones. Like you. The ones who know things, see things, feel things. He needs them. Needs the transfers."

Transfers? Gifted powers?

The evil pressed in, but again she shoved it back. "Transfers?"

He looked back up at her. "The transfer of power helps him. He should be here. He'll be back soon. He needs your power to get better."

They were all fucking nuts.

"But I don't want to give him my power, Jay."

He only stared at her. "They never do."

Her blood iced and she could only stare into those weird eyes, her body starting to tremble.

"H-how does he...does he transfer their power?" She swallowed and focused on him, on her question—and suddenly she saw.

Saw through eyes, so many eyes, so many fears.

She sucked in air or tried to, could all but feel the hands around her neck, squeezing, squeezing.

Oh God. She tried to shake the images off, but they mercilessly sliced into her. Screams echoed in her mind.

Screams. Gasping breaths. Begging. Pleading.

So many of them all but roaring against her mind. All wanting...air, power...life!

No! No! No! She wasn't going to let these monsters win, wasn't going to let them take from her what was hers and only hers.

The trembling shook her so that the entire bed trembled but still she stared, saw what had been done, what could be done, what would be done to her if she didn't get the hell out of here.

❧

Max slammed to a stop at the mouth of the alley that led to the bookstore. Even as he was depressing the locks on the doors, the Crown Vic pulled to a stop behind them. Agent Morrow climbed out.

"Can't have you running out on your own."

Max's fear and anger lashed out at the man. "I don't give a fuck what you think you can or can't have. I'm going to find my daughter."

He walked to the door, tried it. Damned thing was locked. Not waiting for the agent, he bent down, and picked up a rock. With all the fury roiling inside him, he hurled it against the old glass panes.

Glass shattered in the oncoming dawn.

"That was great! Want another rock?" Lake asked him.

He knew she was trying to distract him, but he ignored her.

"Sorry," she said. "Let's go. I've never broken and entered before, at least not that I'll admit to."

Without another word to either her or Agent Morrow, he reached in and unlocked the damned door. He paused and looked at the next building. As with many of these old buildings, they were butted up against each other. However, he knew enough about old Taos to know that those were newer additions. Most had had very narrow alleyways between some of the buildings.

Instead of entering, he walked on around the block and down the side of the building. He jogged to where the bookstore ended. Sure enough, on this end of the building there was an alleyway between the two buildings, big enough for maybe him and Lake to fit side by side. The wall was midway down the store. Storage?

Hurrying back around, he calculated where the wall between would be. Once he was back at the entrance, he saw that both Lake and Agent Morrow had already gone inside.

"Wall's been added," he told them.

"Yes, we know. There is a connecting hallway between this building and the next."

He shook his head. "Too big and long for only a hallway." He realized that the brothers had lived in the building next door. Hallway?

He studied it. He opened all the doors along the hallway. They were all closets.

But something tugged at him as he neared the one next to the end on the left. He closed his eyes and thought about where the wall was in the alley, where it ended. Not here, it was further down, much further down. So what was the extra space?

For the first time in his life, he tried, honestly tried to *know* with that part of him he'd all but ignored for his forty-two years.

Something inside him shimmered, flickered and then went out.

He felt Lake beside him. She didn't say a word, but he knew *she* knew he was trying.

"You can do this..."

Could he? He looked at her.

"I believe in you. I believe in me. We'll find her."

Yes, they would.

Alyssa gasped for breath and shook her head, trying to rid herself of the images. All she could see was face after face, most of them young girls, all of them wanting her help.

Help.

She wanted help.

Dad...

And then she felt him. "Dad," she whispered and then started to yell it, her focus centered within herself.

Hands wrapped around her throat.

"I can help him. Help my brother," the voice whispered against her cheek.

She blinked, ripped away from the image of her father standing with his eyes closed, and stared into the yellow eyes of Jay.

His hands, those long-fingered hands were so tight, tighter...

She trembled and tried to fight him off. He pressed her back against the bed. With her hands pushing and shoving against him, she didn't have time to catch herself.

He was on top of her.

No. No. No. She'd be damned if she died like this.

"We need your power," he said, his voice hoarse.

She shook her head and beat her hands against his

shoulders, but it did no good.

Something hit the wall from the other side, thundering through the room, and Jay looked over his shoulder, his attention momentarily turned from her.

This time, she cupped her hands and slammed them against his ears.

He howled.

The wall trembled and she focused on the door, trying to get away from the man trapping her on the bed.

He climbed off her, looked from the wall back to her and then to the corner beside him.

He jumped over the bed and turned to her. She scrambled back and fell off the bed, still trying to get air into her lungs, gray spots dancing in front of her eyes.

"I'll be back for you." He walked into the corner. Or around it? Into it? He was just gone.

Gone.

Where the hell did he go?

The door burst open.

"Alyssa!"

She could only stare at the corner. Where did he go? Where?

God, she could still feel his hands, so tight around her throat. No air...trying to breathe...trying to...

Hands gripped her shoulders, her face... She saw her father talking to her, but she couldn't hear him.

The world faded around her.

Epilogue

Three weeks later

He stopped at the edge of the road, wondering where he was. Where was his brother? The car was warm, but then so was the weather this far south. South. He liked the South. Reminded him of what it was like before. Before, when his brother was with him.

Part of him missed his brother. His brother had always, always taken care of him. Now, he took care of himself. And he liked it.

He liked his life.

He liked his power.

He liked finding power.

He shuddered and wondered where he'd go next. Who he'd find next. What fun they might share.

And he thought of her.

Alyssa.

He would come back for her. One day. One day. One day...

Alyssa stared out her bedroom window. Three weeks since

the attack. Three weeks since one brother slipped into a coma and one escaped to God knew where. Jay. Jay gave her nightmares. She could still see those strange eyes staring at her in the dead of night when it was too quiet and she thought too long on what could have happened. Thanks to a secret door in the corner of the room from hell, he'd slipped away before her father had broken through the hidden door in a closet.

Three weeks and yet it seemed like last night, or a year had past. The bruises had faded around her neck and she at least sounded normal now. But things were far, far from normal.

Where before she saw a few things, or knew a few things, saw auras... Now? Now she saw too much, felt too much, knew too much. There were the dreams, which sometimes showed her things that ended up happening. That was weird, but nothing new. The intensity of the dreams was, however. Now walking by a building and seeing people who she knew no one else saw was becoming normal, or at least not surprising. There was also the fact she could look at someone and know things about them. Gave a whole new meaning to too-much-info.

Some might call it cool.

She figured she was cursed.

Her father was worried about her, Mark was too nice to her and Thad hadn't talked to her in weeks. Which was fine with her. The fewer people she had to interact with these days, the better. She'd seen Murbanks just the other day when he came in about the showing next month. But even the excitement that had once been there now dimmed, with all that had happened. He was still nice, but he understood. She respected him for it.

So now she painted. Painted and painted. She rarely thought about what she was working on, or how it would turn out. She just painted.

The images were rarely pleasant, though sometimes they

were. Sometimes. For the most part, they were dark, grisly scenes that she showed to no one. Her father had seen them, cocked a brow at her and only said, "Have you mentioned these to your parapsychologist?"

Yes, she had. She'd sensed the doctor was more excited over the increase of power or extra gifts she might have than what her subconscious picked up. One of the scenes had already been proved to be a crime two states away.

Lovely. Freak show, that was her.

She glanced at the long counter running down the side of the studio and saw the giant Murbanks.

And she'd never been on her date. Then again, that just seemed like a hassle. Not that she expected Jonathan to ask her out again, and if he did, she'd turn him down. She was busy discovering Alyssa, who—she was honest enough to admit—was one weird girl.

She cranked the music and kept painting, wondering how her father was faring in Sedona.

Sedona, Arizona

Max walked into the building, the bell above the door dinging. Lake, her red hair slipping from her braid, stood behind a counter, boxes stacked everywhere. "I'll be with you in a sec."

She was jotting something down on a piece of paper. Plastic wrapping lay over one side of the counter. Tapestries and wraps hung from the ceiling in various styles and colors. Celtic, African, Indian work.

Eclectic to say the least. He absently picked something up

and realized it was a deck of tarot cards.

He waited.

Finally, she raised her head, "What can—" A huge smile broke over those sexy lips. Lips he hadn't kissed in weeks.

She shoved a wayward strand of hair out of her face. The long red curl would be as soft as silk and smell like apples.

"What can I do for you?" she finally asked, leaning up on the counter so that her ample cleavage was framed in her scooped top.

He was so weak.

Slowly, he let his gaze rake back up to meet her eyes. "Oh, I can think of a few things."

"Promise?" She licked her lips.

He smiled and leaned on the counter as well, meeting her almost halfway across. "Actually I came here for a reason."

"Uh-huh," she whispered, her eyes dropping to his lips. "And what would that be?"

"To bring you back to Taos," he told her, leaning even closer.

That damned smile... "Yeah, well, I was heading out there this weekend. I've almost got everything packed up."

He frowned. She leaned closer and licked his bottom lip. "I sold my shop here. And bought one in Taos."

"You did?" He started to pull back, but she cupped the back of his head.

"Surprise."

He laughed. "Ever amazed."

She met him, the kiss turning wild.

"Did you lock the door?" she asked between nibbles.

"No."

"Should probably do that."

"Yeah. Probably."

"So you were coming to Taos?" he asked, as he broke the kiss to walk to the door. He flipped the closed sign and hit the light switch. Late afternoon light dimmed the shop.

She only grinned. Minx.

"You could have told me." He'd stayed away, kept his distance.

She crossed to him. "But where's the fun in that?"

"I'll show you fun," he said looking down into her face. He wrapped his arms around her, jerking her close.

"Promises, promises."

About the Author

Sometimes people grow up and sometimes some of us only partially grow up. As a child Jaycee had imaginary friends and worlds. She, like everyone else, assumed she'd outgrow it. Now she knows her friends grew up with her and want their stories told. When she's not plotting murder and mayhem, Jaycee tries to keep up with her boys, stay ahead at work, and make certain her assignments in communications and science disorders are turned in on time. She does have to take breaks from all the above for the really fun stuff like laundry, dishes and yard work.

Jaycee lives in Texas with her family, two cats, two corgis and a fluctuating number of betas.

To learn more about Jaycee Clark, please visit www.jayceeclark.com. Send an email to Jaycee at jaycee@jayceeclark.com or join her Yahoo! group to join in the fun with other readers as well as Jaycee at http://groups.yahoo.com/group/jayceesden.

GREAT
CHEAP
FUN

Discover eBooks!

THE FASTEST WAY TO GET THE HOTTEST NAMES

Get your favorite authors on your favorite reader, long before they're out in print! Ebooks from Samhain go wherever you go, and work with whatever you carry—Palm, PDF, Mobi, and more.

WWW.SAMHAINPUBLISHING.COM

LaVergne, TN USA
18 June 2010
186604LV00002B/26/P